"Have You Received So Few Compliments In Your Life?"

Garret reached out to pluck a pink wildflower one of the children had given her from Laura's hair, and he smiled crookedly at its thistlelike stem. "This suits you. Tempting but prickly. How's your patient?"

"Do you really care?"

As she made an attempt to step past him, he caught her arm. "Laura, I'm trying to make polite conversation."

Tossing her braid over her shoulder, she glared up at him. It wasn't her wisest move. Standing this close, she was reminded of how tall and powerfully built he was, and how vulnerable she'd felt in his arms.

"Why haven't you left?" she whispered, furious at herself for the betraying tremor in her voice.

"My generous host made me an offer I couldn't refuse, though I can't say much for his choice of menswear," he drawled, indicating the oversize shirt and dove-gray slacks. "What do you think?"

"I think if there was an ounce of decency in you you'd go away and leave all of us alone."

Garret's hold on her arm tightened in warning, but his expression remained congenial, if slightly mocking. "All of you—or just you?"

"Don't flatter yourself, O'Keefe. I built up an immunity to men like you a long time ago."

Dear Reader:

Six down, six to go... It's July, and I hope you've been enjoying our "Year of the Man." From January to December, 1989 is a twelve-month extravaganza at Silhouette Desire. We're spotlighting one book each month with special cover treatment as a tribute to the Silhouette Desire hero—our *Man of the Month*!

Created by your favorite authors, these men are utterly irresistible. One of Lass Small's Lambert sisters gets a very special man in July. *Man of the Month* Graham Rawlins may start as the *Odd Man Out*, but that doesn't last long....

And Mr. August, Joyce Thies's *Mountain Man* thinks he's conquered it all by facing Alaska, America's last frontier—but he hasn't met his mail-order bride yet!

Yours,

Isabel Swift
Senior Editor & Editorial Coordinator

HELEN R. MYERS
The Pirate O'Keefe

Silhouette Desire

Published by Silhouette Books New York

America's Publisher of Contemporary Romance

SILHOUETTE BOOKS
300 East 42nd St., New York, N.Y. 10017

ISBN: 0-373-05506-4

First Silhouette Books printing July 1989

Printed in the U.S.A.

Books by Helen R. Myers

Silhouette Desire

Partners for Life #370
Smooth Operator #454
That Fontaine Woman! #471
The Pirate O'Keefe #506

Silhouette Romance

Donovan's Mermaid #557
Someone to Watch over Me #643

HELEN R. MYERS,

formerly from New Jersey, met her husband, Robert, a Washington native, in Texas and decided the state was indeed a place for new beginnings. Today they live deep in the piney woods of East Texas, making pets of everything that comes to the front pasture. Her hobbies remain anything that doesn't require a needle and thread, but she admits that writing all those stories cluttering her mind is a priority she can live with.

For Bobbie, Margarett, Carol and Pat
and all the members of RWA-ETC.
Thanks for your friendship and support.

Prologue

He was in trouble. He'd been eager to get away from Miami, he'd pushed hard, and now what was his reward? An unexpected storm that threatened to destroy his boat. As *Thetis* rolled crazily beneath him and the wind roared, sounding like all the demons in hell moaning at once, the truth was a heavy weight in his chest. The pressure built as he fought to keep the craft from capsizing. He wished he could seek release in a scream or curse or prayer. But there wasn't even time for that; there was only time for frantic work and concentrating on survival.

And where was he now, anyway? He hadn't looked at a gauge, compass, or map for longer than was comfortable. Knowing he was somewhere between Grand Bahama Island and the Abacos was hardly reassuring. Somewhere out there were coral reefs and cays, nasty surprises to the ignorant or unsuspecting sailor. Trouble. How was he, often dubbed the *Golden Boy*, the *Man with the Midas Touch*, going to get himself out of this one?

He should never have pushed so hard, but that was as senseless as saying he should never get tired. Excess had always been a problem of his. He worked hard and he played hard, and a few days ago when he'd decided he'd had enough of boardrooms—and, yes, even bedrooms—he'd boarded *Thetis* in Miami and sailed hard to get away from it all. Single-mindedness—that's what it all boiled down to, and hadn't enough people warned him that one day he would pay for having too much of it? He'd always laughed it off; he wasn't laughing now. God, had he ever been through a storm like this one before? Maybe, but never in a craft this small.

Even as he thought that, another wave rose before him like a black mountain and *Thetis* valiantly rose at the stern trying to scale its crest. But the sleek forty-footer was no match for the raw tonnage blasting her; she hovered in the air, a lance caught between centrifugal force and gravity, then fell, rejected by the elements.

His stomach lurched, but the resulting strangled curse was obliterated by the roaring wind. Off balance, he lost his footing and, with his full weight, fell over the wheel. Pain shot through his chest and his breath rushed out in a groan.

Before he could even think of regaining control, *Thetis* caught a smaller wave on her port side and went into a roll. He felt the deck swing out from beneath him and groped desperately for the wheel, but it, too, had taken on a life of its own. Spinning madly, it slapped at his fingers until they were numb with pain.

Continuing its roll, *Thetis* tossed him against the starboard bulwark and, as he suffered a blow to his spine, he heard something that made his blood turn cold: They were on the reefs!

"*No!*" he screamed, scrambling to grab the wheel again.

But it was too late. The boat was slit open like a gutted fish. The force of the blow sent him overboard along with everything else that wasn't strapped down. As he hit the water, he felt the life jacket, which he'd never had time to secure, half rip from his body. The tortured gnashing of forced joints and the sounds of fractured beams joined the deafening cacophony of the storm. There was nothing else to do but get away from the area; if he didn't, he would surely be killed by the churning wreckage.

He swam with one arm, the other holding desperately to the buoyant vest, kicking frantically, his panic finding some useful outlet. All the while, between spitting out mouthfuls of tepid saltwater, he gasped for precious air. It occurred to him that he should be grateful he was sailing in warm seas, but for the moment his gratitude was in short supply. Nowhere could he spot a sign of land or another boat; it was raining too hard; the waves were too high. Within moments, he even lost sight of *Thetis*. He would never have believed she could go down that quickly.

Was that it then? Was this the way it was going to end? Sweet heaven, he might have had a full life, but he wasn't even forty yet! He'd heard it said that when a man faces his own death, his life flashes before him; however, all that was racing through his mind was the reminder of things he'd *never* achieved—the damnedest things, like carrying a bride over a threshold and holding a firstborn. All right, so maybe it was his own fault that he'd struck out there; and maybe he'd been deluding himself when he'd insisted his life was complete without all that. But now that he was faced with the probability that it was lost to him, *he wanted it*. Missing out on those things was going to bother him—more than losing all the money and everything. Why hadn't he tried harder? Why hadn't he ignored some of his innate suspiciousness and tried?

He never saw the wall of water that struck him and sucked him under; he only felt the blow. It made him irrationally, wonderfully furious. Even as he felt himself churned like all the world's dirty laundry in a giant washer, even when his leg slammed against something sharp and he experienced an excruciating pain, he was furious. And he began to fight his way back to the surface.

Not yet, he thought, feeling the pulse of the sea pounding in his ears. Not yet, he insisted as his lungs threatened to burst in their demand for oxygen.

He shot to the surface. His first gasping breath was the angry roar of an injured beast.

"Not yet!" he shouted into the darkness.

One

"Only one sucker, Butch," Dr. Laura Connell said, trying hard not to laugh as her patient stuck his hand into the candy jar capturing all his chubby fist could hold. "Have a heart. Don't you think it would be nice to leave something for the other children?"

"No."

She cleared her throat to hide an escaping chuckle and glanced over the top of the child's head at his mother. "You know, Mrs. Joseph, on second thought maybe his rash might clear up a lot faster if I *did* give him a shot."

The boy's heavily lashed eyes grew wide and, with a shrewdness that belied his youth, he quickly narrowed his choice down to one candy. "Look, Dr. Laura," he cried, almost hitting her in the nose with it. "A green one."

"Wonderful, sweetheart. But I thought orange was your favorite?"

"No, *green* like de crawlies."

As he ran off laughing, Laura exchanged dry looks with his mother, then put the candy jar back on the counter. "If you ever manage to catch up with him, try to put on some of that ointment I've given you say—three times a day." She scribbled a few notes in his file. "I'm sure you'll see an improvement shortly."

She followed the younger woman out of the reception room where she found three more people waiting. What was going on? she wondered. Had an epidemic hit the island? Usually she could count on her weekends being free, unless there was an emergency. But then there was no telling what these islanders constituted an emergency.

The one rule that applied on the island of Big Salt was that no rules applied. Meals were eaten when there was hunger, work was done when there was an inclination to do it, and bills, Laura thought dryly as she watched Butch's mother pay half of what she owed, were always negotiable. It was a different world from the one she'd been used to when she first came here five years ago, and it had taken some adjusting to acclimate herself. But now it seemed, despite all its eccentricities, the sanest place on earth.

She owed Mo lunch for coming in and helping her on what was also supposed to be his day off, but as she glanced at her watch, she saw it was already close to noon. Lunch would have to wait a while longer.

"Well," she said, sitting down on the edge of Mo's battered army-surplus desk and smiling at her three patients. "Who wants to be my next victim? Miss Jewel, what are you doing out in this heat without that umbrella I gave you?"

"Forgot it, Doc," the old woman replied, giving her a gap-toothed grin.

More than likely she'd lent it to one of her grandsons and he'd broken it while playing paratrooper, but Laura couldn't bring herself to scold her. Miss Jewel's heart was as kind as it was frail.

"Elias wants his cast removed," Mo told her, indicating the short, stocky man sitting in the corner who'd fallen out of a mango tree a few weeks before and broken his arm. It was to Mo's credit that he managed to maintain a straight face because every week since, Elias had been showing up on their doorstep asking if it was *time.*

"Sorry, Elias," Laura said patiently. "It's still too soon."

"I come back next week."

"Not next week, either. I told you when I put on that cast that it would take a minimum of six weeks, possibly more."

"Itches, Doc."

Laura removed the stethoscope hanging from her neck and slid a hand beneath her braided hair to massage her nape. "I imagine it does in this heat." Her own white cotton shirt and khaki slacks already felt damp and uncomfortable. "Did you try dusting a little of that cornstarch I gave you in there? Usually that helps."

Elias shot a quick look at the others before dropping his gaze to the tile floor. "Gina put it in de soup."

If it wasn't such a common response, and such a tragic one, Laura would have been tempted to laugh. But there was nothing funny about being poor and she'd learned never to be surprised at anything these people did to make ends meet.

She turned to Mo. Maurice St. Jacques was a perfect example of the potential these islanders could realize if opportunity would simply present itself. Soon after arriving here, she'd discovered he had a gift, not only for learning but for compassion. Raised by his grandmother, one of the few islanders who'd had some schooling, he'd come to Laura to offer his services at whatever handiwork she might need done in exchange for lessons. Now, at twenty, he was her right hand and even assisted her in simple operations.

"Mo, why don't you take Elias into the back and see what you can do to relieve his discomfort. Then give him another box of cornstarch to take home. I'll see to Miss Jewel and Uncle George. Elias," she added quietly as the embarrassed man shuffled by her. "Tell Gina to save you a little next time, okay?"

"Yes, Doc."

Laura went over to sit down beside George, Miss Jewel's husband, and patted his wizened hand. "What brings you out from under your shade tree to disrupt my day off, old man?"

"Got a tooth ailing me, Doc."

"A tooth? Lord, I swear you were put down here to keep me on my toes." Sighing, she reached into her shirt pocket for her penlight. "I tell you I'm not an optometrist and you come in here blind as a bat and asking for glasses. I tell you I'm not a dentist and you come back with a toothache. Open wide."

"You got to pull it, Doc," Miss Jewel said, clasping her husband's other hand. "He say if you don', he going to tie it to de back of Mr. Barnaby's Jeep an' wait."

Laura made a small ceremony of clicking off the light and replacing it in her pocket. "I don't know if I'd risk that, Uncle George. You know Mr. Barnaby has a tendency to shift into reverse about as often as he does first gear."

"Take my chances."

Certain that the two of them had plotted their strategy on the way to her clinic, Laura didn't let them down by giving in too easily. Even on Big Salt there was a social decorum to follow. An idea, no matter how impossible, had to be considered with respect.

"All right," she said at last. "I agree it has to come out, but because I'm still treating you for anemia, the only thing I can give you is a little island rum to deaden the area. Is that acceptable, Miss Jewel?"

It was common knowledge that Miss Jewel didn't like her husband anywhere near spirits of any kind, but it was a different story when it was for medicinal purposes. Resigned, she nodded her head.

"Might need a little to ease de pain later, too," George murmured to Laura as she helped him to his feet.

"Don't push your luck, you old rogue. The last thing you want me to do is make a mistake and pull the wrong tooth."

In the end, Uncle George decided he would need several cotton balls soaked in rum before he would let Laura work on him, and it was close to one o'clock before she and Mo once again found themselves with an empty clinic.

Laura brought out sandwiches and iced tea from her connecting apartment, as she usually did for lunch, and they ate at his desk while updating their patients' files. Actually Mo did the catching up. He enjoyed paperwork, and his writing was far more legible than Laura's. But while he did that, she kicked back in one of the metal chairs, hoisted her legs up on the edge of the desk and, nibbling halfheartedly on a chicken-salad sandwich, worked on the monthly supply list she had to turn in to Barnaby Tremaine.

Medical supplies had been guaranteed by the island's owner when they'd first discussed her taking the job. All she had to do, he'd assured her, was provide him with a monthly list and he would take care of the rest. "I want my people taken care of," he'd stated in one of his early letters to her. "Their welfare is important to me."

"Humph. Maybe when you're sober," she muttered under her breath.

"What's that, Doc?" Mo pushed his glasses back up his nose and trained his eager brown eyes on her.

She smiled wryly. He never failed to make her heart melt, no matter how tired, depressed, or frustrated she became. It had nothing to do with the perfection of his bone structure beneath his ebony skin; Mo was beautiful on the inside. Hope radiated from him like a beacon; he exuded compassion. As hard as she'd worked to attain her degree, had she ever had half his spirit? Maybe. Once.

"I said you can have the other half of my sandwich." She popped the last mouthful of the first half into her mouth and quickly swallowed it, grimacing. "And let's not take any more chickens as payment for a while. Okay? I still have six in my freezer that I'm considering donating to Elias and Gina."

There was no fooling Mo and he surmised her real thoughts quickly. "You always *did* hate making out that list."

"Because he'll take forever to get it filled and then only bring me part of what I asked for." But she also added a crooked smile. "You have to stop reading me so well. At your age it's darned spooky."

"And what *you* have to do is go on vacation."

"Don't be silly. I'm already in Shangri-la. White beaches. Crystalline water. Flowers to make your heart break—"

"An' if dey don' de poverty will," Mo drawled, slipping into the island patois he'd worked hard to overcome. "We're beginning to tire you out, Doc. You need a break before you grow to resent us."

"Remind me not to lend you any more of my psychology textbooks." Straightening, she dropped her sandal-clad feet to the floor and laid down her pad. "What I *resent* is our benefactor's inability to maintain his sobriety, as well as my not being able to do everything for you that I know I could had I a little more support."

"You're missing your cheeseburgers, Doc."

"Yes, well, I'm human. And you'll understand the fixation once you've tasted one." Someday, somehow, she would see that he did. She shoved her plate toward him. "Now eat this before we have to put another notch in that belt of yours."

They were just cleaning up when a small band of children came chasing into her yard, then through the open doorway. Excited and filled with self-importance, they all tried to speak at once.

"*I* found him."

"Musta been de storm washed him ashore."

"I thought he was dead."

"Not dead, stupid, he's sleep'n. My father said so."

"Hold it," Laura said, raising her hands to signal for quiet. "Everyone calm down and let's back up. Angel." She nodded to the tallest boy in the group, the one who'd announced the find. "You're the eldest, why don't you tell me what's going on."

The lanky teenager proudly thrust out his bony chest. "We was beachcombing, see'n what de storm washed up."

"Were," Laura said, automatically correcting him.

"Aw, Doc, not now. How am I gonna tell you if'n I gotta concentrate on what I'm say'n?"

"Practice makes perfect. Besides, didn't I tell you it's important to set an example for the children?"

He glanced down his nose at the others. "Hear dat? *She* even called you children. Next time I tell you who's de boss, you listen."

"Angel, can we hold the indoctrination classes for another time?"

"What?"

"Get on with your story."

"Yes'm. Anyway, we saw a mess of stuff downbeach by Crab Cove and dat's where we found him. Big guy. All cut up and just laying there."

"Dear Lord. Let me get my bag and you can take me to him."

"Don't have to," Angel replied, before she could take two steps. "We got Shrimp's father and uncle to carry him here."

Seconds later the sound of a donkey braying led everyone outside and Laura saw the two men had loaded the stranger onto the back of their cart to bring him the half-mile distance. Small wonder, she decided. Seeing the length of legs dangling over the end of the wagon made her realize Angel wasn't exaggerating this time; their charge *was* a big man.

With Mo and the children following at her heels, she rushed toward the cart and, giving the two men a cursory nod, went straight to her new patient. Angel hadn't been exaggerating about the injured man's condition either; he was a mess, and his slacks—all that was left of his clothing—were nearly shredded. That gave her a clear view of the six-inch gash on his right thigh, and knowing how much blood he could have lost from it, she quickly felt for a pulse. He was alive. He was also a stranger to the island. No one here had a mane of hair and full beard that caught the sun like burnished gold.

"All right," she murmured. "Let's get him inside before the sun finishes what the sea obviously started."

"Better let us carry him, Doc," Shrimp's father said, rounding to the back of the cart himself. "He was almost too much for me'n Jimbo to handle."

Eyeing the unconscious man's pallor, Laura shook her head. "Mo and I will take his legs. If that wound starts to bleed again, there's a good chance he could go into shock or suffer heart failure. On the count of three, gentlemen..."

At five-eight, and with her active life-style, Laura considered herself strong; but even with the man's weight distributed among the four of them, she felt her leg muscles tremble under their share of the burden. Still, when she heard the man's deep groan, she dismissed her own discomfort and refocused on him. "Hold on," she murmured urgently. "We're going to get you inside where I can examine you. Try to hold on a few more moments."

They proceeded to carry him across the yard and through the waiting room into the large back room that served as both surgery and patient ward. The examining table was in actuality a gurney. Once they managed to get him on it, Laura slumped back against the wall to catch her breath.

"My God, he's solid muscle," she gasped.

Thanking Angel and the others, she ushered them back through the waiting room and out the front door. Then she hurried back to her patient where Mo was scrubbing his hands in preparation to assist her.

"Where do you suppose he came from?" he asked, making room for her to join him at the sink.

"I don't know, but it must have been a rough ride." When she finally approached the table and began her examination, she verbalized her findings so Mo could record them for their files. "Looks like we have a contusion on the upper left *frons*," she said, carefully examining the swelling on his forehead. She took out her penlight again and, lifting his left eyelid, then his right, checked the dilation of his pupils. "Some indication of concussion," she murmured, unable to help noticing Nordic blue corneas. "One, two...possibly four bruised ribs. Darn, I wish I had an X-ray machine. Will you look at this leg. No knife did that."

"Coral," Mo told her. "I've seen wounds like that before. Do you suppose he was trying to sail through that storm last night and ran into the reefs?"

"It's as good a guess as any. Hand me those scissors and I'll cut away what's left of these pants. The saltwater did a terrific job of cleansing and cauterizing, but then he ruined it all by washing up on the beach. We have to get this sand out and get him sutured before infection sets in."

They worked quickly and efficiently. Only once did the stranger show signs of regaining consciousness and at that point Laura gave him a local anesthetic to ease the pain she knew she would cause with the needle and thread. Then she pressed him back onto the gurney and reassured him with softly spoken words and a cool hand pressed to his full-bearded cheek.

When they had done all they could for him, Laura dropped down onto a nearby stool and ran the back of her hand across her brow. "He'll probably sleep through until tomorrow." That meant there would be no answers to the many questions forming in her mind and as her gaze was drawn back to his face once again, she experienced an odd feeling of restlessness.

"Do you want to move him to one of the beds?"

Glancing around the sterile room, she thought of Lizzy who was due to go into labor at any hour and shook her head. "Let's put him in my apartment. Lizzy's not going to have an easy birth and I want to be able to provide her with as much privacy as I can. Besides, our friend here is too big for our cots."

They rolled him through one doorway and then another until they were in the building's spacious efficiency-style area Laura called home. Here, too, furnishings and appliances had the same questionable provenance as Mo's desk. There was a queen-size brass bed that, judging by its ornamentation, had to have come from a brothel, a dresser that could have belonged to Queen Victoria, some rattan chairs, a couch unworthy of being bought *or* stolen, and the only other electrical appliances on the island besides Barnaby's—a stove and refrigerator. After once making the mistake of asking Barnaby *how* he'd obtained some of her things, she'd learned to accept what he occasionally brought her without asking questions and, except for her medical supplies, never made a request for anything she couldn't order and pay for herself.

After getting their patient settled in her bed, Laura and Mo collapsed in the rattan chairs to recuperate. Half-lowered bamboo shades and opened screened windows offered what little comfort was available against the heat.

"I should stay," Mo said decisively. "You'll never be able to manage him on your own."

"What's to manage? I told you, he'll probably be out until at least tomorrow, so there's no reason why we both should lose out sleeping in our own beds and enjoying a restful night. Besides, I need you to drop off that supply list at Barnaby's and then stop in to see if Lizzy is all right since I won't be able to do that myself."

Satisfied that he could be of further help by following her directions, Mo left a few minutes later. After walking him out, she returned to her private living quarters where her gaze was immediately drawn to the man laying in her bed. A wry smile curved her lips. He looked more ridiculous in that thing than she'd once felt. It was his size, of course, and his compelling masculinity.

Approaching the foot of the bed, she rested her forearms on the brass filigree to study him more closely. Deep in sleep, he was oblivious to the heat, and any pain; the sheet she'd covered him with was still tucked neatly around his waist. Equally white against his bronzed skin were the bandages she'd wrapped around his ribs. He looked peaceful, approachable, even tame. But so did grizzly bears when they were asleep, and there was much about this man that reminded her of a big golden bear.

It had been a long time since she'd felt dwarfed by anyone, yet he'd managed to do it while flat on his back. It wasn't only because he had to be inches over six feet, but because he also had the build to go with the height. She'd even caught Mo trying not to grin as she'd struggled to get those bandages around his ribs.

He was an attractive man, she decided now that she had the time to think about it—disturbingly so. He didn't possess the perfect bone structure that Mo did, but in his own way he was every bit as magnificent—despite the cuts and bruises. Beneath that thick mane of golden hair and beard was a strong, almost fierce face. His forehead was broad and high, giving him an air of intelligence. If that was the case he must be successful at whatever he did because his wide, firm mouth promised determination. His nose was sharp, arrow straight, as were his eyebrows, and on his left cheekbone was a faint, thin scar. It wasn't quite clean enough to have been caused by a knife, but the deepening lines around his eyes and bracketing his mouth made it less noticeable than she gathered it once was.

She wondered about it; she wondered about *him*. They'd found nothing in his pockets to give them a hint as to who he was or where he'd come from, except a single-blade knife. He wore no jewelry, bore no tattoos, and as far as she could tell, he didn't even have a cavity. In other words, aside from the sea, he had no discerning marks. For all she knew he could be anyone, from wanted criminal to priest. The possibilities were endless. Maybe she should have had Mo ask Barnaby to radio the authorities on Abaco just in case; but considering the shape this man was in, even if he *did* wake up, he wasn't in any condition to be a threat to her.

She would wait, she decided. First and foremost she was a doctor. He needed rest and she would see he got it.

Walking around to the side of the bed, she leaned over and felt his forehead. It was warmer than before; that wasn't a good sign. She would have to watch him more closely than she'd anticipated.

On impulse, she lightly traced the scar on his cheek and mused, "I wonder what tale you'll have to tell."

The man's breathing remained unchanged. Sighing inwardly, she went to wash the dishes from lunch and see to her other chores.

Two

By nightfall his fever had worsened. Laura had been sitting at the kitchen table catching up on reading back issues of medical journals when the sound of his shallow breathing and restlessness caught her attention. Hurrying to his side, she felt his forehead and, muttering an oath, reached for his wrist. Not only was he burning up, his pulse was accelerating, too.

She hurried back to the kitchen and grabbed the jug of cold water she kept in the refrigerator, then a clean dish towel. Pouring the water into a stainless-steel mixing bowl, she dropped in the towel and headed back to the bed.

"This is going to be a bit of a shock," she murmured conversationally, as if he could hear her. Firmly wringing out the excess water from the towel, she brushed his hair back from his forehead and laid the wet cloth against his hot skin. Within seconds she could feel heat penetrating through it. "I should have known you weren't going to make this easy for me," she sighed.

Again and again she rinsed out the towel in cold water and gently wiped down his body. When the water grew tepid, she replaced it with more from the refrigerator. She also dissolved two aspirin in a half-filled glass of orange-mango juice and, lifting his head from the sweat-dampened pillow, softly encouraged him to drink.

"Come on.... I know you're getting dehydrated. Taste it. That's right. Good, isn't it? A little more. Let's get all this aspirin into you. It's the only thing I can give you since I don't know what you're allergic to."

On and on she spoke, her voice producing a soothing melody, not unlike Barber's "Adagio For Strings," which was playing quietly on her tape deck. Once, she would have been too inhibited to do that and would have cringed in embarrassment at the thought of someone else listening. But at thirty-five she'd come to terms with who she was and wasn't. She'd paid her dues by anyone's standards and was intent on being her own person no matter how eccentric others might think her.

With that self-confidence had come a better understanding of her sexuality and, as she continued to draw the cooled terry cloth down her patient's long limbs and over his firm muscles, she became aware of and accepted her attraction to him. It was strange, really, because in the past she'd always found dark-haired men more appealing. Absence, she mused, was obviously not the only thing that made the heart grow fonder; apparently abstinence carried its own clout.

It was because he was different, she decided after a moment. She'd always shied away from men who were physically more attractive than she was; who needed the hassle of competing with someone who would rather admire his own reflection in a mirror than watch her? This man was undeniably a superb specimen of masculinity, but he was no pretty-faced Adonis. No, he reminded her of the legends she hadn't thought of since her school days; he reminded her of the father god, the brother of Hades and Poseidon. An artist would understand. This man could have modeled as Zeus.

A woman would feel possessed in his arms, not just held, not simply loved. She shifted her gaze to his hands. They were large, long fingered, well cared for, but with calluses on the palms. Hands like his would make most women feel their breasts were small, but oh, the seductive contrast of having those work-roughened palms and long tapered fingers caressing that most sensitive skin....

As she felt a sudden rush of heat course through her, she shook her head at her fanciful thoughts. "Maybe it's better that you *are* dead to the world," she told him. "I'm not sure that having a lady doctor with a vivid imagination would do much to inspire your confidence right now. But don't worry; by the time you're ready to wake up, I'll be the epitome of professionalism."

It was almost midnight when he finally slipped off to a deeper, more relaxed sleep. By then Laura was past exhausted herself because, like most people here, she went to bed early and rose early. She gladly turned off her tape deck and the hurricane lamps she preferred to use instead of the more unreliable electricity. Then she stripped down to her tank top undershirt and matching cotton panties.

Moving one of the rattan chairs closer to the bed, she sat down and stretched out, resting her feet up on the mattress. At least this way, she told herself, she would be awakened if he became restless.

But she needn't have worried. Throughout the night she awoke the moment she sensed his fever returning, and in the faint light of a waning moon repeated the routine of bathing him again and again.

At first light she awoke fully alert, not because she was rested, but because it was her usual time for getting up. Rising, she leaned over and touched her patient's forehead. It was cool.

"Mother?"

Startled, she pulled back, then broke into a bemused grin. *Mother?* "And here I was worried that you might be someone running from the law," she drawled. Well, a criminal wouldn't likely be dreaming about his mother, would he? But that just brought her back to her initial question: who was he? Perhaps he was one of those missionaries that occasionally made the circuit through the islands.

If that was the case, so much for her romantic daydreaming, she thought sighing, unaware of how wistful it sounded; and if that was the way her mind was going to work, then she was in dire need of a strong cup of coffee to get it back in line. Stretching to ease her abused muscles, she rose and padded over to the kitchen to make herself a cup of instant coffee.

Afterward, she carried it to the bathroom where she hoped the combination of caffeine and a quick wash would dispel the lingering feelings of grogginess. Because she had the water running, she didn't hear the man in the bed groan as he woke up. Neither did she see the confusion in his eyes when he opened them and realized that nothing he looked at was even remotely familiar.

Good God Almighty... He felt like someone had taken a meat cleaver and tried to turn him into a veal cutlet. Everything hurt, and what didn't was probably missing.

Cautiously, he closed his eyes to take mental inventory, and remember.

The storm—of course, how could he have forgotten *that*? Memory came quickly and with it the reminder that *Thetis* was lost. He let the sorrow come. Despite what was written about him, he didn't normally feel a strong attachment to personal possessions, but *Thetis* had been special and he would miss her.

Opening his eyes again, he cautiously ran his hand over the two places that hurt the most, only to find both his ribs and his right thigh bandaged. Someone had been working on him, but who? This was obviously not a hospital, he thought glancing around the room. It was— he focused on the brass footboard of his bed with the cherub balancing on the foot of a harp. *Where the hell was he?*

The sound of running water caught his attention, and then the subdued sound of a woman humming. He *knew* that voice—at least he thought he did.

He began to raise his head, to sit up, but pain, a blinding sheet of white—obliterating his vision and totally weakening him—made him drop back against the pillows. He lifted a hand to his head and found a lump the size of a golf ball. A parting kiss from *Thetis* no doubt.

Out of the corner of his eye, he noticed a movement and gingerly turned his head to glance across the room toward the dresser, an heirloom if he ever saw one. There she stood, perfectly reflected in the gilded mirror, bent from the waist and brushing a wonderful cascade of lush reddish-brown hair. Her face was hidden from him at the moment, but that was all right, he decided, because studying the rest of her was more than compensation.

She was long legged and lithe, a bit more more slender than he preferred a woman to be, but the fluid grace with which she moved made that inconsequential. As he considered her underwear, the hint of a smile tugged at his lips. No way in hell it would ever pass for lingerie, but somehow on her it looked sexy. At any rate, it didn't hide the fact that she had a cute bottom and small but firm breasts. She didn't look exactly athletic, but she was in good shape.

When she tossed her head back and her hair settled like a mink cape over her shoulders, he felt something inside him warm, curl, and settle. Nice, he thought, narrowing his eyes with growing interest. Hers were dark, maybe gray or brown, dominating a makeup-free oval face, and they were accompanied by a straight, no-nonsense nose, and a generous mouth that hinted of a contradicting vulnerability. Now he saw that she was a bit older than her body suggested, but he still guessed she was only in her early thirties. She was also a far cry from the glamour queens that had somehow annexed him like a piece of prime real estate, but he liked that, too.

She finished brushing her hair and he watched her exchange the brush for a mug, lifting it to her lips as she turned to leave the bathroom. It was at that moment she looked into the mirror and their gazes locked.

Laura almost choked on her coffee. "You're awake!" she cried, quickly moving around the bathroom door. She set her mug on the bedside table, then sat down on the bed near his hip. "How do you feel?"

"Like a whale chewed on me for a while and spit me out."

As she checked his pulse, amusement replaced some of the concern reflected in her eyes. They were dark brown, he discovered, with flecks of amber in their depths giving them a jewellike quality.

"Ah, so *that's* who you are. Well, congratulations, Jonah; considering your remarkable age, you're in terrific shape."

The attempt to lift an eyebrow cost him and he grimaced in pain. "So are you," he muttered, deciding he liked her voice. It wasn't exactly husky, but it reminded him of hushed whispers in the dark. His own sounded as though he'd taken up smoking again.

She chuckled throatily. "Uh-huh. I obviously remind you of your mother."

"Pardon?" While she checked the bruise on his forehead, she explained what he'd said in his sleep. "You're right," he replied sheepishly. "It must have been the fever talking."

"No problem. I thought it was rather sweet. So who are you? When they brought you here yesterday, you weren't carrying any identification."

She didn't know. Despite his condition, he found the idea of meeting a complete stranger oddly appealing. It was the only excuse he had for wanting to prolong the experience.

"Who are 'they'?"

"The islanders who found you. Well?"

"What? Oh." He hesitated a moment longer. "Garret...Garret Edmund. What's yours?"

"Doctor will do," she replied, reaching for the stethoscope she'd left on the bedside table.

He smiled faintly. "I must be dreaming."

"You'll come out of it when I give you a needle."

"Then may I extend my compliments to whoever designs your uniforms? I have to tell you they're a vast improvement over the things you people usually wear."

Satisfied that his heartbeat was near normal, she removed the instrument and laid it back on the table. "I see

I don't have to worry about that blow to your head affecting your eyesight."

"No, I'd say the eyes are working fairly well."

"So is your mouth."

His blue eyes twinkled in appreciation at her dry wit. It would seem that the lady wasn't a pushover. He liked that even better.

"What *can* I call you besides doctor, Doc?"

"The name's Laura. Laura Connell." She touched his ribs. "How does this bandage feel? Too tight?"

"I'll let you know after I get used to the feeling of having my ribs knocked in. What's wrong with my leg?"

"You have fourteen stitches in it. The cut wasn't neat, but I tried to sew it where there'd be a minimum of scarring. Still, it's not as if it'll be your first, is it?"

"Why, Laura, have you been taking inventory?"

"All in the name of science, Mr. Edmund."

"Call me Garret." The urge to slide his fingers into her hair and draw her close so that he could taste her lips was strong, stimulated by her fresh scent. She smelled of soap and talcum powder, and he realized it appealed to him more than expensive perfumes. "Could I have a cup of whatever it is you're drinking? My throat feels like a sewer trench."

"Of course—and I'm not surprised. After swallowing half the saltwater in the Caribbean and then burning up with fever, you're also dehydrated. But coffee is out," she murmured, rising and heading for the kitchen. "Do you remember what happened to you?"

"More or less. I got caught in a storm and my boat went down."

"Were you alone?" she asked, immediately concerned for the fate of anyone else who might have been on board.

"Yes. By the way, where am I?"

"Big Salt."

He recalled having seen the name on a nautical map. It was one of the islands in the pearllike string he'd sailed past dozens of times, but never bothered to stop at because they were very little fish in a bountiful sea. "Unusual name. Is that supposed to be an axiom of some kind?"

"Reverse psychology. The original settlers wanted to keep the paradise they'd found to themselves and named it that to suggest the water supply was terrible. It's the same premise they used in naming Greenland and Iceland."

"Did it work?" he asked, watching her stretch to reach up into a cabinet for a juice glass.

"Only too well. Barnaby Tremaine is the last descendant of those original colonists. When he dies, the island will probably be placed under Abaco's administration because he's never married and there are no heirs. The others who live here are all share croppers on his estate and I don't know what will happen to them. I suppose they'll stay until they're evicted."

"And you? What will you do?"

She shrugged and filled the glass with a pale orange concoction she took out of the refrigerator. "I haven't given it much thought. I suppose I'd return to the States; though it's been a while since I've been back, and I'm not sure I'd care to adjust to all the rules and regulations that go along with working at a big hospital. I came here from Philadelphia," she explained, returning to his side.

"It certainly would put a damper on your mode of dress." With her help, he eased himself farther up on the pillows and then gratefully accepted the glass she handed him.

"Does my appearance bother you?"

"Not if it doesn't bother you."

"I'm a doctor," she reminded him, retrieving her own mug and heading back to the kitchen to make herself another coffee. "The human body is hardly a mystery to me. Besides, I'm wearing more than they do on some resort beaches and, in case you haven't noticed, this place isn't air-conditioned."

"Feel free to remove anything else you find oppressive."

Laura glanced over her shoulder and eyed him speculatively. "I think you're a flirt, Mr. Edmund, and it's only fair to warn you that I'm not. Nor am I susceptible to smooth talkers."

Though she spoke quietly, even amiably, he sensed a hint of tension in her and wondered what, or rather *who* she'd been burned by. "Warning noted, Doc. I'll do my best to think of you as fat, homely, and wearing surgery scrubs, but if I happen to slip once in a while, just shrug it off as a side effect of the fever."

"Oh, brother."

Not wanting to give her time for more of a comeback, he held up his nearly empty glass. "This is interesting; orange-and-mango juice, isn't it?"

"Very good, but take it easy with drinking it too fast. You can get just as sick from overdoing it." She returned with her steaming coffee and set it back down on the bedside table. This time she sat down on the chair she'd slept in, then reached for the pencil and pad of paper beside her mug. "Why don't you tell me who you'd like me to notify? We don't have any telephones on the island, but Barnaby keeps a shortwave radio up at the main house. He can contact the authorities on Great

Abaco and have them phone or wire your family to let them know you're relatively all right.''

"I don't have a family."

Laura glanced up from the pad, drawn by the somber tone of his voice as much as by the revelation of what he'd said. She found herself searching his face, looking for the answers to questions that came unbidden and all too quickly. It seemed impossible that a man like him— so full of life, so confident—would be completely alone.

"Surely, there's *someone*?" She gave him a faintly reproachful smile. "What about that mother you mentioned in your sleep?"

"She's been gone for years."

But he still missed her, or why else would he have been dreaming of her? "Your father, perhaps?"

"He's gone, too, and even if he weren't, I wouldn't have recommended you contact him. We were never that close. And no, before you ask, there are no brothers or sisters."

A part of her—she supposed it was her latent maternal instinct, or the part that had eventually led her to be a doctor—felt a tug of compassion. But the worldly-wise and cautious side warned her not to let down her defenses too easily. It was that side she chose to listen to.

She lifted her chin and pressed on determinedly. "Well, you work, don't you?"

The hint of laughter returned to his eyes. "Some people might want to dispute that, but, yes, I work."

"Doing what?"

"This and that. Right now I'm . . . in between things." He sipped the last of his juice and gingerly placed the glass on the bedside table.

Seeing what the effort cost him, Laura put away the pad and pencil and helped him slip back down into a more comfortable position. "This is why I want to notify someone for you. You're not going to be in any shape to do much of anything for several days. If there's someone who might be waiting to hear from you, it's only fair that we let them know you're all right."

"Everyone knew I was going to be . . . inaccessible for a while," he replied, feeling a lethargy overcome him, despite the amount of sleep he'd had. He looked up into Laura's dark eyes and decided things could have turned out a lot worse. "Looks like you're stuck with me, Doc."

"Lucky me."

Even as his eyes began to grow heavy and close, the corner of his mouth twitched. "I'll grow on you."

"I can't wait." Giving in to impulse, Laura brushed a lock of golden hair off his brow.

"Hey, Doc?"

"Hmm?"

"I've been meaning to ask, where'd you get the crazy bed?"

"Mona's Massage Parlour. They were having a going out of business sale."

"You're a real comedian."

"Yeah. But I'll grow on you."

"I think I like the idea of that."

Three

When she was certain he'd dropped off to sleep again, Laura collected both her mug and his glass and quietly made her way to the kitchen. There she made herself her last cup of coffee for the day and, while drinking it, studied the man in her bed.

He wasn't at all what she'd expected; in some ways he was more. She'd expected the confidence; the sensitivity was a surprise—an appealing one. Like her, he was alone in the world, and like her, he tried to hide that sometimes he got lonely.

She liked him, despite her reservations and wariness, despite his tendency toward outrageous flirtation. She liked him.

But, she reminded herself, he was clearly a drifter. In a short time he would be back on his feet and then he would be gone. If she became tempted to like him too much, she would do well to remember that.

She was grateful it was Sunday, reliably a quiet day on the island, unless it was the first Sunday of the month when the visiting missionary came to hold outdoor services. The islanders always honored the visit with a lavish cookout, but Mr. Goodwyn had come last week. That meant she would have plenty of time to keep a close eye on her patient.

Her only visitor that morning was Mo, who'd conscientiously come to see how she was coping. After she let him see for himself that everything was fine, she gave him another textbook to read and sent him on his way.

Living alone, she rarely went to too much trouble in preparing meals for herself; but Garret Edmund was undoubtedly a man with a healthy appetite and she knew that when he finally woke up completely, he would probably be ravenous. That prompted her to defrost one of those normally dreaded chickens, cut it up, and in the early afternoon put it on her small grill out back. The aroma must have been halfway decent, for soon after the wind shifted and carried the scent of pineapple and chicken through the opened windows, he roused.

"If that tastes half as good as it smells, I think I'm in love," he said, spotting her at the kitchen counter.

Ignoring the tiny rush of excitement his words had inspired, Laura turned from the tomato salad she was preparing and sent him a mild look. "You'll probably want to wash up before you eat. Hold on a moment and I'll help you to the bathroom."

"I'm banged up a bit, not disabled." He flung the sheet away and swung his legs to the floor. At least he thought he did—his body protested and the pain was blinding. When he was able to refocus again, he found Laura leaning against the brass bedpost. He decided to ignore the attractive picture she made with her breasts resting against her crossed arms, and focus on the suspiciously benign expression on her face. He could almost hear what was going on inside that pretty head of hers: *Ah, the ego of the macho male.*

Sighing, he wiped at his damp brow. "I hope you're not going to be one of those people who like to say, 'I told you so.'"

"Half the process of healing is the patient's willingness to do so." She moved around to his side of the bed and, easing herself under his arm, carefully helped him to his feet. She was wearing shorts and, with him in only his briefs, their thighs were soon pressed together as intimately as lovers. "I'll try not to hurt you but let me know if I move too fast."

"Shouldn't that be my line?"

"I'm going to ignore you if you don't behave."

They inched their way across the few feet to the bathroom. Garret kept his mind off his pain by concentrating on the way her hardening nipples thrust against her navy tank top, but by the time they reached the bathroom door he decided the tactic had worked too well and eased himself away from her.

"I think I can manage from here."

"All right, but don't get any ideas about taking a shower. You'll have to settle for a sponge bath for the next few days until I take those stitches out."

"Do you have a razor I can borrow or are those smooth legs of yours waxed?"

"In the medicine cabinet. Don't slip," she muttered, closing the door with a little more force than necessary.

His answering grin disappeared the moment he was alone. He rested the bulk of his weight against the sink to maintain his balance and closed his eyes. God, he hadn't felt this bad since he'd tried to outswim that shark while scuba diving off the Keys and got the bends from surfacing too quickly. Of course, it had been preferable to being lunch to the shark; just as this was preferable to being with *Thetis* on the bottom of the Caribbean.

Life was indeed sweet, and it was made sweeter by the presence of Laura Connell. She was a bonus he couldn't possibly have anticipated, and though he sensed she was equally attracted to him, he was aware she was resisting it. Cautious lady. The question was, was it a natural reaction to strangers, or something that went deeper? Whatever the reason, he wasn't in any condition to do anything about it—*or* his healthy hormones for that matter. For the moment, at least, the lady was safe.

A half hour later, Laura glanced at the cooling dinner she'd prepared and started to worry. He certainly was being quiet in there. What if something was wrong? What if he'd fainted while she was outside getting the chicken? He could be lying on the tile floor this very moment bleeding while she stood around worrying about offending his pride.

"Oh, hang your pride," she muttered, heading for the bathroom.

The door opened as she was reaching for the knob and she had to jump back to avoid being struck. When she peered around it, she saw that her worst concerns had almost materialized; he'd pushed himself to his limit and beneath his tan his skin had a gray tinge.

She moved quickly to act as a crutch under his right arm, but her exasperation was evident in her look and her voice. "It wasn't enough that you had to be big, you have to be stubborn as well. Why didn't you call me?"

"I needed to get cleaned up."

"A presentable corpse would still be a corpse, Mr. Edmund."

"Hell, where'd you learn your bedside manner? I thought you people were supposed to be compassionate."

"We leave that to the nurses. A doctor's priority is to keep the patient alive," she snapped back, for a moment ignoring what she knew was an invaluable asset to both professions. When she'd finally managed to get him back into bed and had the sheet tucked up around his waist, she straightened and allowed her sympathy to surface because he really did look terrible. "I'm sorry for scolding, but you should have called me. If you reopen that wound, or start to bleed internally you could die before I could get a medical helicopter from the main island to fly you to a fully equipped hospital. Please remember that in the future. I may be a doctor, but there's only so much I can do with the equipment and supplies I have."

This was more like it, he thought basking in the warmth her brown eyes generated. He might be more accustomed to giving orders than taking them, yet there had been a few exceptions in his life. What he'd never experienced before was having a woman read him the riot act. He respected her spirit, just as he respected her professionalism, but he preferred the Laura Connell he was seeing now—warm, and softer.

"Would you like to rest awhile before you eat?" she asked, growing a little uncomfortable with the way he was simply watching her.

That snapped him out of his daydreaming and he gave her an aggrieved look. "Doc, if I don't eat soon, I'm going to need a safety pin to hold up these skivvies."

"Right." She cleared her throat. "Well, let me get your tray."

Though still weak, he ate his dinner with relish. Laura placed her own plate on a TV tray and sat down nearby to keep him company. In order to keep him from wolfing down his food, and to appease her own curiosity, she kept him preoccupied with questions about himself.

"Do you think your boat's a total loss?"

"*Thetis* came apart on the reefs. She's probably scattered for miles by now." He frowned and touched his chest, then thought about some of the handcrafted nautical equipment he'd been carrying that had been a gift—and a particularly old bottle of Napoleon brandy. "If something *did* happen to wash ashore here, do you think your islanders would bring it over?"

"Depends on what it is. If it's food rations or clothing, you might as well forget it. But if they recognize it as something obviously expensive, they'd probably bring it. By and large, they're an honest bunch." She scooped her rice into a more compact mass with her fork. "*Thetis* is a lovely name; it comes from Greek mythology, doesn't it?"

"She was one of the Nereids, mother of Achilles."

"A sea nymph who gave birth to a mortal.... The children would love that story, and there are some here who'd suggest history had repeated itself. I'm surprised there hasn't been a parade of visitors at my door wanting to see the golden-haired giant the sea cast onto our beach."

"If they do come, I trust you'll inform them that I'm indisposed?"

By his expression, she could tell he was serious and her initial curiosity and wariness returned. He could be simply antisocial, she tried to reassure herself, a man who simply preferred to live and work alone. Yet she didn't think so. After all, he clearly enjoyed talking to her.

Talking, yes, but saying little.

"You're American, aren't you?" she asked.

"Yes."

"Have you been away for long?"

"A few days."

"Oh. Where'd you put out from?"

"Miami."

"Is that where you live?"

"Sometimes. This is very good. Do you grow the pineapples here on the island?"

"No. We trade tomatoes and bananas for them with another island. Was this a vacation for you?"

"Partly."

"I hope you had sufficient insurance on your boat."

"I don't think I'll have any complaints. How many people live on Big Salt?"

"Just under a hundred."

"And most of them are islanders?"

"All of them except for me."

"What made you decide to come here?"

Laura put down her fork and took her time to take a drink of her iced tea. "I was in a rut. I needed a change and when I saw Barnaby's ad I decided it was what I'd been looking for." That was close enough to the truth, she decided and gave him an exasperated look. "You're not supposed to be asking the questions. *I* am."

"How else am I supposed to get to know you."

"I'd prefer to get to know *you* first."

"Trust me," he said with a disarming smile. "I make boring copy. A couple of times a year I leave my mundane office job and sail around a bit." He lifted one corner of his mouth in lieu of shrugging, indicating it was no big deal.

"On the contrary; *doing* is much more impressive than staying at that office job and only *dreaming*."

"Maybe, but you're the one who had the nerve to go after what you wanted one hundred percent. It must have taken a tremendous amount of courage to leave your home, family, and a reliable job to come to a tiny place that doesn't even exist on most maps."

If only he knew, thought Laura. It had been a relief. She had been at the point where if one more person had asked her about her broken engagement, or had given her one of those sympathetic looks, she might have shown them that Dr. Connell was hardly the quiet mouse they all believed her to be.

"I don't have any close family, either." And the aunts, uncles, and cousins she *did* have must have sighed in relief when they received her notes advising them of her decision to move. When she'd left, none had shown up to say goodbye. "So you see, I'm hardly what you could call courageous."

"Do you miss the States?"

She missed something—but what? Mo had been right the other day when he said she was getting tired, yet it wasn't of Big Salt. Never had she felt she belonged more to a place and its people. From the beginning, they had accepted her, and while she liked to believe her presence had made a difference to the general welfare of the islanders, they had made a difference to her, as well. They had reestablished her belief in herself, reminding her that it wasn't a person's lineage or wealth that was important but who they were on the inside.

"Difficult question?"

She refocused and found him watching her intently, but from beneath low, hooded eyes. "This has worn you out," she replied instead, putting aside her tray to rise and take his. "You can have dessert when you wake up again. Are you allergic to any type of medication? I want to give you an antibiotic for your leg."

"I'd prefer dessert."

"It will be in pill form not a needle."

"I'm not fond of pills, either."

"Well, at least you're running true to form." After setting the tray on the kitchen counter, she reached into her medical bag on the table and took out a small brown bottle. "I've yet to meet a man who wasn't a trying patient."

As she returned to the bed to hand it to him along with more juice to wash it down, he closed his hand around her wrist. "It's a personal quirk of mine," he insisted, his voice low but firm. "I have this thing about losing control."

She glanced down at the big hand gently holding her wrist. There was no doubt in her mind that if he wanted to, he could snap it with very little effort. Lifting her gaze back to his, she gave him a dry smile. "Tell you what. I'll wait to take advantage of you until you have a fighting chance. How's that?"

After the slightest of hesitations, the amusement returned to his eyes. "Doc, where the hell have you been all my life?"

"Just take the pill, Mr. Edmund, and then go to sleep. I could use the break."

But as she filled the dishpan with soap and water minutes later, Laura discovered that a smile lingered around her lips. It had been a long time since she'd been paid *that* kind of attention, and though she assured herself that she was fully aware it was only meant to be taken lightly, she was enjoying it. Why not? she decided with an inner shrug. After all, she was a normal, healthy female and they were both single. As long as it went no further, what harm could it do? Humming under her breath, she reached for their drinking glasses and lowered them into the water.

He slept through the night and when he opened his eyes the next morning, the first thing he saw was Laura sleeping on that sorry excuse for a couch. Curled into a fetal position because it was too short even for her, she looked appealingly tousled and approachable. It made him feel guilty for taking up her bed, but there was contentment, too.

As if she felt his intent study of her, her eyes opened and for a moment she stared at him as though he were a stranger. Then recognition registered and, blinking, she checked her watch.

"Oh, blast," she muttered, bouncing off the couch with a speed that was a holdover from her intern days when forty-hour shifts were the norm, and ten minute catnaps were all that kept her functioning for days on end. "I can't believe I could oversleep on that relic. Has there been anyone knocking on the front door? Darn, I have exactly twenty minutes to shower, make breakfast, and get out front."

"Good morning to you, too, Doc."

Laura froze at the bathroom doorway, slacks and shirt in hand, and peered around the bathroom door. "Sorry. Good morning. How do you feel?"

"Much better. What's the rush?"

"It's Monday."

It didn't take long for him to realize the implications of that. Mondays were predictably busy for her. It was the day her elderly patients came to visit her, whether they needed medical treatment or merely an attentive ear, and it was the day when she saw people from one of the neighboring islands, as well.

Garret soon discovered he'd grown accustomed to having her around, and when she *did* come in the back, either to look for something or check on him, he found himself trying to delay her by involving her in conversation. But he was never very successful and he found himself actually annoyed when she sent her young aide in her place.

It was late afternoon when she returned and announced she thought she was through for the day. She poured two glasses of iced tea and, handing one to Garret, dropped with a sigh into a rattan chair.

"This is usually my busiest day of the week, barring any emergencies on other days, but it's been a while since we've been this hectic. I'm afraid I lost a few points with some of the children; several needed tetanus shots."

"They're lucky to have you," Garret said, changing his mind about telling her that he disliked iced tea and would prefer a beer.

"If only they could afford shoes," she mused, barely hearing him. She shook her head and began unbuttoning her shirt, completely oblivious to the way his gaze followed the progression of her fingers. "How are you doing? You must be starved by now. Give me a minute to catch my breath and I'll start dinner."

"Relax. I can wait."

Giving him a grateful smile, she smoothed her glass across her already damp forehead. "Oh, I almost forgot. One of the children who found you the other day brought in a metal box. It had been inside one of those airtight plastic coolers, which is why I suppose it didn't sink. Does it sound like yours?"

It was where he kept his extra cash and his passport, among other things. And it was always kept locked. He wondered if it still was.

"Yes. I appreciate the kid's honesty. I have a few dollars tucked away in there in case of an emergency. Tell him he can have the cooler if he has a use for it."

"I already did," Laura replied with a grin. "They've been finding a few other things, but mostly bits and pieces of the boat. I've been told the wood is of very fine quality, so I hope you won't be expecting any of it back. Lumber's worth a premium around here."

They talked more as Laura changed into shorts and prepared dinner, a fruit salad for herself and broiled pork chops with steamed vegetables for Garret. The pig who'd donated the chops, she told him cheerfully, had also been island grown.

Laura barely had the dishes washed when she heard someone out front. It was Lizzy, the young pregnant woman she'd been concerned about, and she was in her first stages of labor. Laura briefly explained the situation to Garret and set her tape deck nearby where he could reach it.

"It's going to be a long night, and probably not a pleasant one. If it gets to be too much for you, play this as loud as necessary to drown out her screams."

At first, Garret thought the remark a bit melodramatic; after all, women had been having babies for centuries. It might not be the easiest of experiences, but could it be that bad?

Seven and a half hours later, he found himself reaching for the tape deck. Sweet Jesus, he thought, could anyone stand so much pain and survive? Could he continue to listen and not go out of his mind?

Just as abruptly, he withdrew his hand, instead wiping it across his sweat-dampened forehead. No, if she could take it, the least he could do was keep quiet. The poor woman probably thought she and Laura were alone in the place; maybe she would be embarrassed to know someone else was listening to her agony.

It lasted nearly another hour, and then there was a different scream, more of a deep-bellied moan that could have come from a man. Finally silence, strange and eerie, filled the room, followed by a pitiful wail. Garret found himself breaking into a wide, foolish grin, and wondering if the baby was a boy or a girl.

A few minutes later the door leading to the clinic opened and Laura entered the nearly dark room carrying a tiny blanketed bundle in her arms. She gave him a rueful smile.

"I thought you might still be awake. Would you like to meet the newest member of our community?"

As she sat down beside him on the bed, he gazed at the miniature, wrinkled face with the tightly closed eyes. It was hardly what he would call a pretty sight, and yet there was something endearing about the little thing.

"It's so tiny."

"So's the mother."

"What is it? I mean is it a boy or girl?"

"Girl. Poor Lizzy. She was hoping for a son, thinking that it would make a difference to her boyfriend. It won't, but I didn't want to take even that dream away from her."

"Is she all right?"

Laura was silent a moment. "She'll pull through."

She left to put the baby in a crib near her mother. When she returned to her apartment, she took a quick shower and changed into a fresh pair of briefs and a T-shirt.

"You must be exhausted," Garret said, watching her put the tape deck back on the kitchen counter.

She got herself a long drink of ice water from the refrigerator. Then she refilled his glass in case he woke up thirsty and brought it to the bedside table. "I almost fell asleep in the shower," she admitted, reaching for the light switch.

"Wait." He reached out, touching her arm. "Sleep here. There's room for both of us. You can't get any rest on that thing over there."

Laura stared at him for several seconds before his invitation sank in. She glanced at the empty side of the bed, which suddenly didn't seem as roomy as he suggested. But on the other hand it was more space than she would have on the couch. Still, *sleep* with him?

"I don't think...I mean, I might accidentally hurt you," she said, looking for a graceful way out.

"You're dead on your feet. You won't budge. Here, lay down." Without giving her another chance to resist, he drew her awkwardly across him.

"I would have walked around the bed," she muttered.

"Liar." He turned out the light. "You would have run off to the couch, knowing I couldn't bring you back."

She glared at him in the dark. In the morning she would explain to him that she didn't care to be bullied in her own home, but for now, she thought, burrowing deeper into her pillow, for now she would let him get away with it.

"'Night, Doc," he murmured—and waited. "Laura?"

There was no reply, only the sound of her quiet breathing.

He smiled and closed his own eyes.

* * *

She thought it would take Mo pounding at the front door to wake her again, but when Laura opened her eyes, it was barely dawn, and decidedly quiet. She lay there for a moment wondering if she could afford to allow herself another fifteen or twenty minutes. It was relatively early and she still felt exhausted from last night, or more accurately this morning. Chances were things would be relatively slow in the clinic today and—*last night?*

She stiffened, her senses sharpened as she remembered. Was he still sleeping? she wondered. Would she have time to slip out of bed before he woke so there wouldn't be any awkward moments? Her back was to him. She couldn't tell.

Slowly, she eased herself onto her back, careful not to rouse him, and found herself looking up into clear blue eyes that held a decided gleam.

"Morning," he murmured with a lazy grin. "Sleep well?"

"I usually do in my own bed."

His eyes twinkled with laughter. Shifting carefully, he let his elbow bear the brunt of his weight and rested his head on his palm. "Full of pepper and vinegar even in the morning. You're a challenge, Laura Connell."

He might as well have traced a finger down her body for the way his eyes did a slow, thorough inspection. It made her feel warmer than the already-warm room did. She tried to convince herself her feeling was indignation.

"Well, you're not. You're predictably obvious, so hold that saccharin-sweet tongue of yours for someone more gullible and I'll get up and make us some coffee."

"Hold it." He lightly pushed her back against the mattress. But there wasn't a trace of the annoyance she'd expected to see on his face, only wry tenderness. "Why are you trying so hard not to like me too much?"

Was it that obvious? Feeling guilty, she glanced away. "I don't dislike you. I'm merely trying to maintain a suitable doctor-patient relationship."

"Darlin'," he said, affecting the hint of a brogue. "Have you ever heard the tale of the little boy whose nose grew longer with every fib he told?"

As he ran his finger down the length of her nose, Laura compressed her lips to keep them from twitching. "You're a real pain in the—"

"Ah-ah-ah."

She exhaled in exasperation and gave in to a slight smile. "Okay, you've made your point. Now can I get up and get that coffee?"

"After you say, 'Garret, you're really a nice man and I'm glad you were beached on my island.'"

"Don't hold your breath," she replied, but the effect was ruined because she was laughing.

Garret chuckled, too, then sighed, his gaze wandering over her face. "Ah, Doc . . . maybe it's a good thing I'm in this condition."

As she met his solemn look, Laura's laughter diminished to a wistful sigh. Her throat grew dry. "Maybe so."

Something hardened in his face, yet when he reached over and ran his thumb across her lower lip, his touch was tentative. "I need to know something," he whispered gruffly, staring at her mouth. "Is there someone—someone special in your life?"

"No."

The word was barely spoken, but he heard and took a deep, careful breath to temper the sense of satisfaction and urgency it gave him. Slowly he began to lean toward her. "I think that's about to change."

She knew of people hearing bells when they kissed—or was it music?—but never a baby crying, and never *before* the kiss had even begun! Then she realized where the sound was coming from.

"It's the baby," she said, wriggling from beneath him and off the bed. "Guess you'll have to wait a while for that coffee."

For other things as well, he told her with a look. But the time would come.

Because she knew he was right, she ran like hell.

Four

She wasn't a coward; she was out of practice. Laura told herself that again and again, and by Wednesday she was almost ready to believe it. The fact that Garret made her feel things with an intensity she'd never felt before had nothing to do with it. Maybe.

"Nuts," she muttered, as she pricked her index finger on a thorn from one of the pale pink rosebushes cascading over the white picket fence in her front yard. She switched her shears into her gloved left hand, already holding two branches of the delicately scented blooms, and lifted her bleeding finger to her mouth. Not even as an intern had she been this clumsy. She didn't know why she was cutting the things, anyway. They never lasted half as long in a vase as they did on the bush, and when was she in her apartment long enough to enjoy them? She was either in the clinic, making calls, outside in her yard, or on the beach.

But deep down she knew the question was an unnecessary one. She hadn't cut the roses for herself; she'd cut them for Garret. He'd been confined to bed for five days now, and it was obvious frustration was setting in. Was boredom also the reason why he was treating her as if she were the first woman he'd seen in years?

Sighing, Laura looked out beyond the path leading down to the beach and gazed wistfully at the ocean; it shimmered with the brilliance of a blue topaz in the mid-morning sun. That's what really had her nerves tying themselves in knots, she told herself. It wasn't the waste of a few blossoms, nor was it the idea of giving up her own bed. It was Garret, and the tiny voice in the back of her mind that kept warning her he was too good to be true. Even as her heart and body yearned to discover the passion his eyes promised, her mind held her back. That's why she'd insisted on returning to the couch after that one night of sleeping with him.

She needed a little more time. It wasn't that she was a prude; for goodness sake, she was thirty-five, and if she wanted to have an affair, then she would. But she had to be sure it would mean something. That didn't mean she was looking for commitments; first of all it was too soon to even think in those terms, but she *was* looking for compassion. Sexual gratification wouldn't be enough. She needed to know that he really cared for her as a person and that she wasn't just a body. And she was looking for honesty. Perhaps more than anything else, she was looking for that. But beneath the passion she saw in Garret's eyes she saw secrets—and so, she resisted him.

What could he be hiding? she wondered. If only she could look inside that metal box, she might discover the truth. Yet Garret seemed in no hurry to open the thing. She could still ask Barnaby to radio the authorities on

Abaco, but she hadn't seen *that* scoundrel in days, which could only mean one thing: he was recovering from another drinking binge. It made the corners of her mouth turn downward.

She supposed she'd better check on him later, after she stopped by to see Lizzy, who'd gone home with her baby yesterday afternoon; because she knew if Barnaby was seriously ill, Sarah, his housekeeper, would have already sent for her. While she was there she might go ahead and ask him to radio for news. In the meantime the roses needed to get into water before they wilted in her hands.

She was just walking through the front door of the clinic when Garret appeared through the doorway heading toward the examination room. Dressed only in the shorts she'd made out of his tattered slacks, he looked like a battle-weary Tarzan with his chest and thigh bandaged. By the way he was holding on to the doorjamb, it was also clear he was still extremely weak.

As he wavered, she tossed everything in her hands onto the reception desk and rushed to him. "What are you trying to do, have a relapse or rip open those stitches?" she snapped, pushing him back against the wall.

"Ow! Watch the ribs, will you?" he muttered, grasping her upper arms to help steady himself.

"You should have thought of that *before* you got out of bed."

"I'm sick of being in that bed—especially when you're not around."

Laura ignored his coaxing smile and raised a hand to touch his forehead. "Well, I hate to have to break this to you, but I do have other things to do besides— Now, look what you've done. Your fever is back."

"I love it when you try to hide your concern for me, Doc."

"If you pass out on me, how am I supposed to get you back into bed?"

"Just put my head in your lap and let me die a happy man."

"Will you please be serious!"

Garret narrowed his eyes. "Serious, huh? Okay. How's this?"

He slid one hand to the back of her head and closed it around her braid, tugging it with gentle insistence until her head fell back. Then he claimed her mouth with his.

Surprise ricocheted through her along with indignation, and desire. He wouldn't, she thought; he couldn't. But he did. He kissed her with the hunger of a man fully capable of following it through to a satisfying completion. With his lips, he teased; with his tongue, he promised, and with his hands he held her prisoner until she was weak-kneed and almost relying on him to support her.

"Was that serious enough for you?" he whispered gruffly against her lips.

She tried to ignore the caress of his thumb along her cheekbone and that she already missed the harder contact of his mouth. "This shouldn't have happened."

"The devil it shouldn't."

"We're strangers. . . . You're ill."

"We've just spent the past five days together—sometimes in the same bed—are you going to tell me that this is coming as a surprise to you?" The words were barely audible as he made a sensuous journey exploring the soft line of her throat.

"No."

"If the baby hadn't cried yesterday morning, that kiss just now would have already happened. Maybe more."

"But you couldn't," Laura said, trying to ignore her racing heartbeat and think as a doctor.

Garret smiled slightly. "Where there's a will..." Then he tilted her chin up, forcing her to meet his intent scrutiny. "Tell me you want me, Laura."

"I wish I didn't."

"That's hardly what I had in mind."

"This isn't easy for me, Garret."

"I know. I think that's part of the attraction. Shall I make it easier?"

Again he took her mouth with his, but this time there wasn't any tentative coaxing, only quick possession, and then a heady rush of hot desire coursing through his veins. He'd already waited long enough to taste her again. Could a man become addicted on one kiss? What a surprise she was. He'd expected to enjoy kissing her, just as he enjoyed looking at her, but there weren't words to describe this response. It was a fever.

He slid his hands down her back, urging her closer, and he almost smiled at how careful she was not to hurt his ribs. How could she match the suggestive stroking of his tongue and yet be thinking of something else? He didn't want her to be able to think at all—except of him, and how good it was going to be between them.

As he urged her hips into the cradle of his, he heard the soft murmur of yearning deep in her throat, and his temperature climbed a few more degrees. "Let's lock the door," he whispered, his hands making a slow journey to explore what before he'd only been able to admire with his eyes. "Let's draw down the shades. We'll undress each other and lay down on that big empty bed."

Picturing it, Laura stroked her fingers through the golden mat of hair covering his chest. "It's so early; someone could come."

"We'll ignore them." He slid his hands up her sides following the indentation of her slender waist and the gentle swell of her breasts. "I want to look at you here, taste you."

"I'm small."

"You're perfect." He slid his hands to the shoulder straps of her navy tank top. "I'm tempted to slide these down right now and prove it to you."

She wanted him to. She wanted to cover his hands with her own and help him. No one had ever made her feel this desired or this beautiful. But as she began to tell him so, there was a roar outside like that of an approaching vehicle and then the squeal of brakes.

"Laura!" A gruff male voice shouted. "Where are you, woman? Someone's told me there's a piece of live flotsam who's beached himself on my—"

Laura sighed and leaned back against the opposite wall, crossing her arms as she watched the man, who reminded her of a dissolute dwarf, jerk to a wobbly halt in the doorway. "He's right here where he has been for the past five days," she replied dryly. "And if you hadn't been busy soaking your liver in whiskey, you would have understood that from the message I gave Mo to bring to you."

He dragged the misshapen lightweight fedora from his head and tried to smooth down the wild tangle of gray hair that framed a shiny bald crown. "Mmm...a note, you say? The lad must've forgotten to bring it."

"Mo is completely reliable, which is more than I can say for some people around here."

The stout little man grimaced, causing his bloodshot eyes to all but disappear, and rubbed at his five-day-old beard. "Not in front of the guest, my dear. You'll have him thinking the worst of me."

"At least he won't be disappointed," she replied drolly, before glancing at Garret. "Meet Barnaby Tremaine, the owner of this questionable paradise. Barnaby, Garret Edmund, your live flotsam.''

Barnaby sent her a baleful look, then shuffled forward, extending his hand toward Garret. "A pleasure, sir. You must ignore our little repartee. I rely on Laura to keep my wit sharp; the truth is I'm as fond of her as I would be of my own daughter, had I been blessed with one.''

"Who can explain the wisdom of divine providence?" Laura drawled.

"Good to meet you," Garret said, stifling a smile.

Having forgotten his glasses at home, Barnaby leaned closer, squinting. "Ah, you're an American, aren't you? How nice for Laura. You know, I sometimes worry— Well, I'll be damned."

"Probably," Laura murmured in agreement. Then she noticed the way Barnaby was staring at Garret, and the wary expression that spread over Garret's face. "What is it?" she demanded, straightening and continuing to look from one to the other.

"Nothing," Garret muttered.

"Nonsense," countered Barnaby. "Do you know who you have here? It's the pirate himself. O'Keefe!''

Laura felt the room sway under her feet. O'Keefe! Who didn't know the name of the man who was almost as famous as some of the privateers who'd once sailed these waters, whose own ship had been called nothing less than a great white shark. O'Keefe—the corporate raider who amused himself with beautiful women and adventures wherever he found them. She'd always thought Big Salt too insignificant to worry that he would come here. What a joke that fate should decide otherwise. No wonder she'd fallen under his spell. But to think she'd almost become another statistic....

"Why this is splendid, splendid," Barnaby said, pumping Garret's hand more enthusiastically. "You're exactly who I need to speak to for some financial advice. Listen up, Laura. That's the other reason I've come down to see you."

Garret could feel the change in Laura like a waft of cold air, but he couldn't begin to guess the reason. "I'm flattered, but I make it a point never to give advice if I can help it."

Laura ignored him and focused on Barnaby. "What are you talking about?"

"Remember those investment people who wrote me several weeks ago? They're coming here next week to look around."

She felt the blood drain from her face and wondered how many other shocks were in store for her; she didn't think she was up to any more. "You know how I feel about that," she replied stiffly.

"It doesn't hurt to listen to what they have to say."

"You promised you wouldn't *sell*."

"I'm not signing anything, my dear, but I'd be foolish not to keep an open mind; after all, I want what's best for the people on Big Salt as much as you do. What I also want is for you to be my guest a week Friday for a dinner party I'm having in their honor."

"Why don't you invite *him* instead?" Laura muttered, indicating Garret with a curt toss of her head. "He's more likely to fit in with the group—not to mention agree with your ultimate decision—than I am."

Garret's eyes narrowed. "A little quick to judge, aren't you?"

"Believe me, I know you, Mr. O'Keefe. Newspapers might be outdated by the time they arrive on Big Salt, but we *do* get them. You buy up corporations just as easily as some people would shoes, and then you dump the ones that aren't profitable because you can make more money by using them as a tax write-off. It wasn't your boat that deserved being called the great white shark, it's *you*."

"I see you have it all figured out," Garret said stiffly. "If my presence has suddenly become so distasteful to you, perhaps Mr. Tremaine can find a place for me elsewhere?"

"Me?" Barnaby glanced from one to the other, trying to keep up with what was clearly over his still-throbbing head. "Oh—yes, by all means. I'd be delighted. Whenever you say, old boy."

"How about right now?"

"Now?" He glanced at Laura and cleared his throat. "Now sounds wise. Have you any luggage to collect? No, of course not. Well, then come along. My Jeep's outside."

Garret turned to Laura, but she refused to look at him. He wasn't surprised; however, it still annoyed him. Little snob. What right did she have to condemn him based on a few newspaper articles? To think he'd believed she was different. He ought to give her a piece of his mind anyway—but then he saw the glimmer of tears in her eyes. Anger, he scoffed trying to dismiss them. She couldn't have the heart for anything else. It could only be anger. Still, he might have died if she hadn't been around to care for him, and for that at least he could show some civility.

"Thank you for your—hospitality, Doctor."

"I assure you, it's no more or less than I'd do for anyone else in your situation."

Knowing he needed to get away from there before he said or did something he might later regret, Garret told Barnaby he was ready to leave and gratefully accepted his aid. They were barely outside when he heard the door to her rooms slam.

"What's her problem?" he asked Barnaby when they were settled in the Jeep.

Barnaby turned the key in the ignition. Gears protested violently as he shifted into first. "Ah, well, she's had something of a difficult life, and I'm afraid when I unwittingly gave away your true identity, it brought it all back."

"Explain."

"You're a reminder of an entire world that's rejected her." The Jeep jerked forward. "You see, she's the illegitimate daughter of Senator John Templeton. The Pennsylvania Templetons? Her mother worked on his clerical staff when he was a freshman congressman. He was already married, had a family of his own, but apparently he convinced her he was serious about her and they had an affair. However, when her mother became pregnant, she soon discovered the true state of his feelings."

"The bastard dumped her."

Barnaby nodded and made a sharp ninety-degree left turn onto the dirt road leading up to his mansion. "She did her best to provide for herself and Laura, but I'm sure you're knowledgeable of what the social ramifications were of having a child out of wedlock back in those days. It was rough for both mother and daughter. She was nineteen when her mother died, but to Laura's credit she put herself through college and then medical school.

"In her second year of residency she met a brilliant young surgeon from a wealthy family. They wanted to marry. But his people wouldn't hear of it and pressured the young man to end the relationship."

Garret swore under his breath—though partly, he told himself, because they'd hit a pothole and he'd taken the jolt all in his ribs. "Talk about getting kicked in the same place twice."

Barnaby grunted in agreement. "Burned her good on men like you—but don't sell her short. She's the best thing that ever happened to this place. God knows, she keeps me from making a total mess of things. She might be a bit headstrong, but it's what we need. Earth mother, that's what she is. You'll understand if you stay around here any length of time."

He drove between two fields where workers were turning the earth in preparation for planting a new crop, and waved his hat in greeting, calling to one or two by name. Seconds later the road became a circular driveway and he brought the Jeep to an abrupt halt before a sprawling two-story frame house.

"Here we are. Welcome to Whitehall. Not exactly as majestic as its namesake, I'll admit, but hell, it's mine."

As Barnaby laughed at the private joke, Garret gazed up at the mansion. Once it must have been a magnificent sight to sailors who passed close to the island, but now it was a ghostly reminder of decayed dreams, its balconies overgrown with vines, the paint peeling, some storm shutters hanging by a single nail.

Easing out of the Jeep, Garret told himself the sooner he radioed his people the better. Chances were if there was an extra bed in this place, the sheets were probably in as bad shape as the rest of the house. Laura probably knew that and even now was having a good laugh at his expense. Well, not for long, he decided, holding the paint-chipped railing to ease up the first stair of the porch. By tomorrow he would have himself off this island

and then Dr. Laura Connell could find someone else to
use as a whipping boy for her misfortunes.

She loved an evening swim when the sinking sun turned
the water into liquid fire, a shimmering sea of orange
flames. It never failed to relieve the tension Laura accu-
mulated from a long day of work. She could float on her
back and watch clouds drift by or swim until her muscles ached pleasantly, then sit on the beach to dry off and
wait for the first evening star to appear.

But not tonight. Tonight nothing worked and the tension stayed.

Laura swam toward the beach and when she could
touch bottom, walked the rest of the way, squeezing water from her heavy braid. Her wet, black maillot clung to
her sensitized body, making her uncomfortably aware of
needs she'd managed to ignore until about five days ago.
Inevitably that reminded her of this morning, and Garret.

O'Keefe, she corrected herself, her mouth compress-
ing into a grim line. Garret had been an illusion, a lie.
O'Keefe was the man to whom she'd opened her home
and with whom she had almost slept.

"Not that you'd have done much sleeping," she muttered, dropping down on her towel.

Sighing, she propped her forehead against her up-
drawn knees. More than anything, that's what bothered
her. She'd almost given herself to the exact sort of man
she loathed. Rich. Successful. Powerful.

"A pirate," she spat out, raising her head to glare out
at sea.

Oh, yes, she knew O'Keefe. Just last month there had
been an article in an old newsmagazine Barnaby had
passed down to her. It was about his latest coup; he'd

acquired a California movie mogul's extensive art collection including two Van Goghs and a Renoir because the owner had just been served with divorce papers and he wanted to liquidate his assets and hide them in a Swiss bank account. The article had featured a photograph of O'Keefe emerging from a limousine with the man's estranged wife, whom he was escorting to a Broadway musical premiere. The only thing the photograph had lacked was a Jolly Roger hanging from the limo's radio antenna.

That's the kind of man O'Keefe was. If he saw something he wanted, he went after it, no matter the cost. He owned more New York highrises than could be counted on one hand. The stock market was like a candy store to him. His life was nothing more than a series of acquisitions, and nothing, not even friendships, were allowed to get in the way.

Well, she wasn't about to be one of them. She'd been used once, but it wasn't going to happen again. Only why, she wondered, closing her eyes, why hadn't she recognized him before she became attracted? It must have been the beard. Though he was a born rebel, often wearing his hair longer than most businessmen would, in the photographs she'd seen of him he was usually clean shaven. The beard had thrown her. It shouldn't have. It made him look all the more like a buccaneer.

"Doc Laura?"

She swung her head to the left and saw Shrimp standing a few feet away eyeing her cautiously. Touching a hand to her chest, she forced herself to chuckle and smile at the small boy.

"You gave me a start, Shrimp. What are you doing down here at this hour? It's almost dark."

"I wanted to show you dis. You think it's his?"

Laura stretched out her hand to receive the heavy school ring on a broken chain. Brushing off the sand, she held it closer and read the markings identifying it as a college ring. Harvard. Only the best, she thought sarcastically, turning it around to look for an inside inscription. Though it was almost too dark to read, she managed to make out the letters well enough. *Garret Edmund O'Keefe*. Half a lie, but a lie still.

"Yes. Sorry, sweetheart," she murmured, handing it back to the boy. "It's his. He's up with Mr. Barnaby now. You'd better take it on up there and then get home. Okay?"

"Yes'm. 'Night."

"Good night," Laura whispered and laid her forehead back against her knees.

Standing at his bedroom window on the second floor, Garret watched darkness envelope the woman on the beach and felt a strange pulling sensation deep in his chest. Damn her, he thought shoving his hands into the pockets of his shorts. What had he done to her other than try to protect himself? Did she have any idea what it was like to wonder, always wonder if someone was after you for something? What? Why? Did she think she was the only one who'd ever been used?

He'd enjoyed being a nobody for a few days. He'd enjoyed watching her attraction to him grow, knowing that it was for himself and not what he could buy her.

But a woman like Laura wouldn't want presents.

So he'd been a little overcautious.

You would have taken her to bed and when you were well enough to travel you'd have left her just like all the others. You're no better than that jerk who dumped her.

At least he wouldn't have made her any promises.

But was he sure about that? He took a deep careful breath and let his thoughts return again to this morning and the way he'd felt when he'd kissed her. His body tightened at the memory. He hadn't wanted anyone so badly since he was sixteen and one of his father's "amusements" had decided to follow him into the cabana by the pool. The difference was there was a sweetness, a touch of vulnerability with Laura. She wasn't the type of women who would give herself casually. And yet, she'd wanted him. She still did, or why else was she sitting down there looking so sad, so alone?

"It's not over, lady," he muttered, shifting to brace his hands on either side of the window frame.

He was going to stay, he decided. At least for a while. There were problems here, and puzzles. When had he ever been able to resist the challenge of either? And he'd amended his opinion of the place; the accommodations wouldn't be too bad. Tremaine's home was far better cared for than he'd anticipated—though credit went entirely to the housekeeper, Sarah, he was sure. He would go ahead and accept Barnaby's invitation after all. Granted, he'd sent word to Giles to come get him, but his assistant was flexible. He paid him to be.

Before he left he would know why those investors were sniffing around, and why Tremaine was contemplating selling his birthright. That situation alone intrigued him. But most of all he was going to satisfy his curiosity about Dr. Laura Connell. *And* he would prove to her he didn't want anything that wasn't on her mind, too.

"No," he murmured, watching her. "It's not over by a long shot."

Five

Five shells and three shells are how many, anyone?" Laura glanced at the half-dozen children sitting on the ground with her. In her arms she held another, Lizzy's baby. "How about you, Angel?"

The teenager scratched the back of his head, his expression thoroughly bored. "Let one of dem answer."

"You're the one who'll be leaving for a job on Abaco before anyone else and I want you to be able to take care of yourself."

"How's counting gonna help me fish or can?"

"If you can't count, how will you know you're being paid properly? How will you know how to pay for the food you'll have to buy? Come on. Be a good sport," she murmured, gently encouraging him. "Show the others how bright you are."

He drew his lower lip between his teeth and frowned down at the pink-and-white shells on the ground. "Eight?" he asked after a moment.

Laura tried not to show her relief. "Wonderful. Okay, everybody, that's all for today." She chuckled softly, watching them react the same way children everywhere did at the end of a class. As they scattered like fireflies released from a jar, she allowed herself a quiet sigh. If only she had more time to spend with them, not to mention better facilities. These haphazard sessions she managed to give them every few days weren't nearly enough.

She glanced down at the infant in her arms, her expression growing tender. "Maybe things will improve by the time you're ready for school. What do you think, imp?"

The sound of laughter caught her attention and she glanced across toward the boxing sheds where crops were washed and prepared for transport. A number of the islanders had abandoned their task of sorting the latest harvest of tomatoes and cantaloupe and were talking animatedly to Barnaby and Garret. Seeing the blond head that towered above all the others, Laura's smile turned into a scowl.

News traveled fast on the island and she'd already heard the excited chatter regarding the "pirate's" intention to stay on. It didn't sit well with her. Why? she wondered, watching him as he responded to something Barnaby'd said. In the two days since she'd all but evicted him from her clinic, his condition seemed to have improved considerably. He might be relying heavily on one of Barnaby's canes, and through his loose-fitting cotton shirt she could see his ribs were still bandaged, but otherwise he looked to be in prime health. She would have thought he would be anxious to leave. Why hadn't he?

As if he could feel the intensity of her stare, he looked up, met her gaze, and subtly inclined his head. She might have nodded back, but he ruined the inclination to be civil by adding a sly wink. Gritting her teeth together, she dropped her gaze to the baby and began some unnecessary fussing with the infant's diaper.

The oversized louse, she thought darkly. She wished he *would* go. They had enough to deal with as it was. No good could come from his staying. Why couldn't Barnaby see that?

"I think she'll be wanting a feeding before dat needs changing," Lizzy said, coming out of her family's house, a dilapidated bungalow that matched the dozen others lined up beside it.

Laura glanced up and gave her a wry look. "I think you're right. Did you get most of your chores done?"

"The wash is hung out back, but dat's about all. Maybe I'll do Mama's mending when I lay de babe down for her nap."

"You should use that time to catch up on your own rest," Laura told her, eyeing the dark shadows under the new mother's eyes. "I know you feel bad because your mother is working hard over in the cane fields, but you're not going to be able to nurse this baby if you're flat on your back sick, Lizzy."

"I got no choice, Doc." The younger woman accepted the tiny bundle Laura placed in her arms, and for a moment her expression brightened. "She's so beautiful. Thanks for taking care of her for me. Won't be long before she's sitting wid de other children listening to you teach."

Laura watched her go back into the house, wishing she felt as enthusiastic about the idea. How much better it would be if the children had a real teacher, and a schoolhouse where they wouldn't be tempted to run off whenever the mood suited them. Rising, she dusted the dirt from the back of her khaki slacks and reached down for the medical bag she'd laid beside the trunk of a palm tree.

"You're a regular pied piper, aren't you, Doc?"

For a limping man, she decided, he was remarkably light on his feet. Ignoring the flurry of nerves that shot through her, Laura gripped her bag more tightly and turned to face him. "Is that supposed to be some kind of crack?"

"Have you received so few compliments in your life that you can't recognize one when you get it?" He reached out to pluck the pink wildflower one of the children had given her from her hair, only to smile crookedly at its thistlelike stem. "This suits you. Tempting but prickly. How's the baby?"

"Do you really care?"

As she made an attempt to step past him, he caught her arm. "Laura, I'm trying to make polite conversation."

Tossing her braid over her shoulder, she glared up at him.

It wasn't her wisest move. Standing this close she was reminded of how tall and powerfully built he was, and how vulnerable she'd felt being in his arms.

"Why haven't you left?" she whispered, furious at herself for the betraying tremor in her voice.

"Barnaby made me an offer I couldn't refuse, though I can't say much for his connections in menswear. He had these sent over from Abaco," he drawled, indicating the oversize white shirt and dove-gray slacks. "What do you think?"

"I think if there was an ounce of decency in you, you'd go away and leave us alone."

Garret's hold of her arm tightened in warning, but his expression remained congenial, if slightly mocking. "Us—or you?"

"Don't flatter yourself, O'Keefe. I built up an immunity to men like you a long time ago."

"To an image, maybe, but not to the man who shared your bed. I'm tempted to prove that to you," he added, tucking the flower back into her hair. "But knowing how involved we're likely to get, I'll wait for a more private moment."

The heat that burned in Laura had nothing to do with the glaring sun overhead. She jerked her arm free of his grasp. "Go ahead and hold your breath."

"Laura, my dear," Barnaby said, hurrying over to them. "Nice to see you two are speaking again. Has Garret told you the good news? He's agreed to stay a while and has offered me his expertise for when those investment people show up. Bloody good of him, wouldn't you say?"

"Oh, *bloody*." Her eyes narrowed as she noted his unhealthy coloring. "Have you been out in the sun all morning?"

He reached into his pants pocket, drew out a handkerchief, and wiped his perspiring face. "Now don't start scolding. It couldn't be helped. I've been showing Garret the island. We've just come back from the cane fields."

"You look like you walked all the way. Where's your hat?"

"Er—it must be back at the house. Damn, it *is* getting rather hot, isn't it? Why don't you ride back to Whitehall with us, and Sarah can make us all a nice gin and— Oh, dear."

"Barnaby!" As the old man blinked dazedly and began to slump, Laura dropped her bag and grabbed him, easing his way to the ground. "Get me some water, somebody, and a cloth!" Without looking up to see if her directions were being followed, she gently laid his head on a patch of grass and began to unbutton his shirt. Then she reached for her bag and pulled out a small bottle of pills. Removing one she gently eased it between the semiconscious man's lips. "Come on. Take it, you old goat. You know what it is."

She was barely aware that Garret had eased himself down beside her. But when the water came and he began to bathe Barnaby's face and chest with the ragged kitchen towel, she shot him a grateful look.

"Is it his heart?" he asked, relieved to see Barnaby's breathing becoming less labored.

"Yes—among other things."

"I didn't know."

"It wouldn't matter if you did. He's habitually self-destructive." She took Barnaby's blood pressure and listened to his heart. When she was satisfied that his condition had stabilized somewhat, she directed two of the biggest men standing nearby to lift him and carry him to the Jeep. "Let's go," she said to Garret. "I'll drive you back. I have to see that he gets into bed."

After the men placed Barnaby in the Jeep, Laura asked them to climb on wherever they could because she still needed their help. As they reached the house, Sarah led them up the double-width staircase to the grandly furnished master bedroom. While she saw to it that the two men were given something cool to drink for their labors, Laura matter-of-factly began undressing Barnaby.

"Now, wait a minute, woman," he muttered, slapping weakly at her hands. "If I'm in no condition to enjoy this, I'd as soon undress myself, thank you."

Laura poked a finger at his bulbous nose. "Listen to me, you old fool. Your clothes are wet and if I turn on that overhead fan, the next outfit you wear will be your funeral suit. Now stop giving me a hard time; I'll leave you with your dignity. You can ask O'Keefe."

Leaning against the doorjamb, Garret gave Barnaby a reassuring wink. "Beats me how she restrains herself."

Laura ignored that and within minutes had the grumbling man tucked under the bedsheet. Again she checked his heart and blood pressure. "All right. You're stabilizing nicely, but you'll have to stay in bed for the rest of the day. Understand? I'll talk to Sarah about your dinner. Where are those pills I gave you?"

"In the nightstand drawer."

"You're *supposed* to carry them with you at all times." She found them and slapped them on top of the table. "And the rest?"

"The rest of what?"

"Your stash. Where is it?"

"I'm really feeling tired, Laura. Would you mind—"

"Barnaby, I know you. There's a bottle in this room, and if you don't tell me where, so help me I'm going straight home to pack my bags."

"You can't. You're under contract."

"It expired two years ago."

He drew his bushy brows together trying to remember. "You're turning into a hard woman, Laura Connell."

"And you're more trouble than you're worth. Now where is it?"

He resisted a moment longer, then reluctantly reached under his pillow and drew out a pint-size silver flask. "I'm surrounded by bossy women," he told Garret as he handed it to her. "Is it any wonder I need an occasional bit of sedation?"

Laura suppressed a smile and closed her medical bag. "Try to sleep now. I'll check on you later this evening. If you're good, I'll let you try to beat me at a game of checkers."

In the hallway she met Sarah and quietly went over what she wanted Barnaby to eat for the next few days. When she handed over the flask, the two women exchanged wry glances.

She was about to follow Sarah back downstairs when she saw Garret rubbing his right thigh. "Is it bothering you?" she asked approaching him.

"Not much."

Aware he was lying, Laura shook her head and gestured to the other doors lining the hallway. "Which one's yours?"

"I said it's no big deal."

"And I'm already here. Now that we have all the small talk out of the way, which one?"

He led her to the end of the hall to the last room facing the front of the house. Painted the same eggshell white as the master bedroom, it was almost as large, the great mahogany bed with its piecrust trim commanding a good portion of it.

"It's not quite the conversation piece yours is," Garret said, catching her fleeting glance. "But it sleeps well. Care to try it out?"

Laura approached him slowly, a cool smile curving her lips. When they stood face-to-face, she tossed her bag on the bed and placed her hands on her hips. "Let's just stick to business, okay? Drop them."

Garret arched one dark gold eyebrow. "I prefer a little preliminary conversation myself." Seeing temper flair in her eyes, he reached for his belt buckle. "It was only a joke. You need to lighten up a bit."

"I have all the comedy in my life I can handle. Sit down. Take your shirt off, too. I might as well check on your ribs while I'm at it."

Sinking to her knees, she resisted temptation and gently removed the adhesive strips that held the bandage to his thigh. She wasn't proud of behaving like a shrew, but he wasn't getting the message; if they were going to be stuck on the same island, she didn't want anything to do with him outside of a patient/doctor relationship. The sooner he accepted that, the less caustic she would be toward him.

She frowned as she examined his thigh. "You've been on your feet too much. The bandage has been rubbing against the stitches and irritated the wound. You're going to have to keep off this leg and elevate it if you don't want to end up with an infection."

Garret paid only slight attention, his focus on the vision and feel of her cool fingers moving over his thigh. Unpampered hands, and yet there was a delicacy to them, a grace that made him burn to feel them touch other places. All of him.

He drew in a deep breath. "I'll camp out on the chaise longue in Barnaby's room; that way he might be more likely to stay put himself. How's that?"

"I'll believe it when I see it," she murmured. But the corners of her mouth curled upward.

"You really like him, don't you? Behind all your tough-guy posturing, you're crazy about the old coot."

"It's not that simple."

"Does it have to be complicated?"

"He makes it that way." Laura paused in unscrewing the cap off a tube of ointment. "This is a beautiful island and it has enormous potential. When I first came here, I was caught up in his dreams for the place. I still am. But I've also learned that Barnaby has an inherent fear of failure and he hides it by not following through on his promises. Then he has to assuage his guilt by hiding in an alcoholic stupor."

"He must be a very lonely man."

"He's a weak man. In itself that's neither a crime nor sin; but he's also the center of authority here, and what he's letting happen to the people who rely on him *is* criminal." She shrugged, too weary to deal with it any further and went back to smoothing ointment on his wound.

"Why do you stay?"

Laura opened a fresh gauze pad and this time used gauze instead of adhesive to secure it in place. "This is home now, and as you said, I like him. At least I like him enough to try to help him. I know what it's like to be alone and afraid."

Finished with his leg, she started on the bandage around his ribs. Garret watched with amusement as she struggled to reach around him with a minimum of physical contact. Instead her breasts kept brushing against his thigh and he had to suffer the reminder that she wore no bra, a fact that was already burned deep into his memory.

"Uh—maybe it would be easier if I were standing," he muttered.

"Maybe so." Was that her voice that sounded so thin? She swallowed and helped him up, though he needed little assistance because he relied on the square bedpost. "Have they been giving you much trouble?"

"What?"

"Your ribs."

He rubbed at his beard to hide a sly grin. "Yeah. I like to sleep on my stomach and it's been hell."

"Just as well. It only gives you a puffy face."

"Being unphotogenic is the least of my worries."

She doubted he could be if he tried. She tossed the elastic bandage on the bed and smoothed her hands over his chest, schooling her features to remain impassive. But there was no stopping her mind from playing devil's advocate and noting the excitement she felt at touching the hard length of muscles stretched over his torso. Nor was there any use in trying to deny the dismay she once again felt when she traced the spots that were bruised and swollen.

"This must have been painful when it happened," she murmured, needing to fill the silence.

"I hardly remember. I was busy trying to save my boat and my life."

He could have died. He almost did. Had he been afraid in those moments alone out there? Did he feel differently when he opened his eyes in the morning, or was he so used to winning that he'd assumed he would again? She'd read theories about that. There was much to be said about having the right attitude.

She gave herself a mental shake. "Have there been any bleeding, convulsions, excessive pain?"

Only now, he thought, feeling the whisper of her breath tease over him. "I'm all right."

"If ever the bandage proves too tight, I want you to come see me." She began to rebind his ribs.

"And only then?"

"Naturally, if there are other complications," she began, purposely misunderstanding.

He laughed, but there was little humor in it. "You're a warm, giving woman—to everyone but me. Why am I being frozen out? Is my wealth more of a flaw than Tremaine's weakness? Does my success make me less of a person than your precious islanders?"

Laura secured the bandage in place before forcing herself to meet his intent gaze. Standing this close she was subjected to the full magnetism he exuded, but to back away would be a sign of weakness that she was sure he would prey on.

"What could I possibly give you that you need?"

Garret let his gaze wander hungrily over her composed face before closing his hands around her waist and bringing her up against his body. "I want you. You want me."

"I was attracted to Garret Edmund. He doesn't exist, O'Keefe."

Her quiet voice ate through his patience. "You want *me*," he said, sliding his right hand upward until he was cupping her breast. He stroked his thumb across her nipple, taking grim satisfaction in the tremor he felt shoot through her. "In the end that's all that's going to matter."

As he lowered his head, she turned hers away, denying him her mouth. But her breath locked in her throat when he countered the move by pressing a series of branding kisses along the vulnerable length of her neck. She closed her eyes and curled her fingers into fists, pushing against his chest to free herself. She despised him for reducing her to this. She despised herself for wanting it.

"You carry the scent of the tropics," he murmured, nuzzling her ear. "The sweetness of the flowers. The steaminess from the heat. The salt from the sea."

"I'm not some island girl that can be swept off her feet with flattery."

He made an impatient sound as he fumbled with the buttons of her shirt. "I half wish you were in a length of cloth. It would be a lot easier to— Ah, Laura. Kiss me."

She gasped as she lost the struggle. His big warm hand slid inside her shirt and closed over her breast, his mouth captured hers. Heat rose, burning the fine threads of her self-restraint, and need flooded her until she was all but drowning in it.

"Damn you," she moaned, pressing closer to take more of the torture he inflicted on her nipple.

His laugh was a rumble deep in his chest and ended when he bit hungrily at her tender lips, then plunged his tongue deep to sate a more voracious appetite. She could protest all she wanted; she would never be able to deny the passion between them. But could he get her to accept?

"I'm only a man, Laura. Only a man."

She wished she could believe that. As she slid her hands deep into his thick mane of hair, she came close. Or maybe only close to forgetting, ignoring for a moment. But the approaching rumble of thunder inched her back from the edge. Not thunder, she realized, going still in Garret's arms. Someone was coming.

"What is it?" he asked, frowning at her sudden withdrawal.

"Don't you hear it? It sounds like a plane." Drawing completely out of his arms she hurried to the window while fumbling with the buttons of her shirt. She opened the double French doors that led to the balcony. "Not a plane, a helicopter," she called above the deafening roar as it began to descend to the front lawn. "I thought Barnaby said those investment people weren't due to arrive until *next* Friday."

Garret limped over to join her, zipping the trousers he'd slid back into, but he only had to glance at the custom-built white-and-gold jet helicopter to recognize it. "They're not," he replied flatly. "That's mine."

Laura twisted her lips into a bitter smile. "One of the rewards of that 'mundane office job' you were telling me about?"

"That has nothing to do with us!" Garret snapped, pointing outside.

Laura went to retrieve her medical bag. "You're absolutely right, because there is no *us*."

She left him, descending the stairs with a rigidity that should have snapped her backbone. As she reached the front porch, a sharply dressed man with pale green eyes topped the last step. Ignoring his quick smile she jerked a thumb over her shoulder. "Inside."

The dark-haired man uttered a surprised laugh and eyed her with both curiosity and undisguised admiration. "Thank you very much, but how do you know who I want to see?"

Charm, she thought gritting her teeth together. God help her, there were two of them now, and on top of everything else this one had an accent. "I'm psychic," she muttered and kept walking.

Six

On realizing he'd allowed his coffee to grow cold for the second time that morning, Garret scowled into the antique china cup in his hand before tossing the contents over the porch railing. He barely missed hitting the elderly man who was giving the overgrown shrubbery its first trim in years. "Sorry," Garret muttered, setting down the cup and pushing away his unfinished breakfast.

Across the table, oblivious to his restlessness, Barnaby beamed as he watched another man rehanging a repaired shutter on the freshly painted house. "Can't believe the change a few days make. Marvelous idea you had about sprucing up the place, O'Keefe. I should have thought about it myself. Thanks to you, too, Giles. I never would have managed to get all that paint and whatnot here in time if you hadn't volunteered to collect it for me."

The dark-haired man who sat between Barnaby and Garret finished lighting a thin cigar before answering. "Don't mention it. When you work for O'Keefe, you learn to be a jack-of-all-trades. Has he told you about the time he decided to try hot-air ballooning? I followed by truck. The thing went down in a prison in New Mexico, and if I hadn't proved to be such an outstanding tracker, I think they'd have been happy to keep him."

Garret settled back in his chair, a faint smile of amusement replacing his frown. "You might also tell him about the time you joined me on *Thetis* when I was looking for that Spanish galleon off the Keys."

Giles cleared his throat before turning back to Barnaby. "My first and *last* voyage," he explained, his enthusiasm far more subdued. "Little did we know we'd anchored where a drug drop was supposed to be made. I still wake up in a cold sweat from that one."

"Why?" drawled Garret, devilry dancing in his eyes. "The coast guard got there in time, didn't they?"

Giles's reply to that was explicit. "You're mad, O'Keefe. My only hope is that one of these days you'll settle down and look for your excitement in raising a few little hellions of your own. I think it's the only chance I have of living to a ripe old age."

"You'd be bored in a month if I did, English."

"I'm thirty-five; you're about to hit the two-score mark; don't you ever get the urge to get off the roller coaster and leave the amusement park?"

Garret looked away and laid his hand on the side of his bandaged thigh. Less than two weeks ago the proverbial roller coaster had sunk, almost taking him with it. It stopped him from making the glib reply he might ordinarily have made.

"Leg bothering you? I would think it's time to take those stitches out," Giles said, adding with a wink to Barnaby. "I could use an excuse to get an introduction to the lovely Dr. Connell."

"Well, you won't get it hanging around O'Keefe," Barnaby told him. "He and Laura can't seem to get along."

Giles lifted an aristocratic brow. "What's this? The woman exists who's immune to O'Keefe? Now I definitely have to meet the lady."

"Keep it up, Channing," Garret growled, shooting the younger man a look that would have sent other subordinates hunting for cover. "You may yet find yourself shipped to the Australian outback scouting locations for a new shopping development."

"Hmm...I've heard Australian women are even better looking than Americans. Why don't we both go?"

As Barnaby slapped at the table, thoroughly enjoying himself, Garret shook his head in resignation. "Never hire someone to be your right hand who doesn't need the money and is a worse flirt than you are."

"Hold on." Giles murmured, rising as he spotted something in the distance. "Isn't that her over there?"

Garret spun around only to have to clutch his side as his ribs protested the abrupt move. Barnaby acknowledged it was Laura and Giles, tossing away his cigar, leaped off the front porch toward the parked Jeep.

"Channing!" Garret shouted. *"Damn it."*

Against her better judgment, Laura decided to take the main road back to her clinic instead of inching her way through the shortcut that was all but overgrown. For the past few days she'd been trying to avoid Whitehall the way the children gave her a wide berth after an inoculation, and except for checking on Barnaby that first night as promised, she'd been successful. But she knew it was ridiculous to keep hiding like a deer sensing hunting season. O'Keefe wasn't going to disappear just because she wanted him to; he was making that clear by the strong show of his influence over Barnaby.

There were changes going on. The island was buzzing with talk about them, and as much as she hated to admit it, the changes were for the better. For starters, Whitehall was undergoing a massive beautification program. Though she'd purposely kept her distance and couldn't appreciate the full quality of the work being done, it didn't take X-ray vision to notice the painting and repairs, the yard work and the window polishing.

But it hadn't stopped there. Barnaby had called several of his most reliable workmen to the mansion and had asked them to do their best to talk to the others and see what they could do about giving the rest of the island a face-lift as well. He'd provided some help: roofing materials for those who went to sleep peering at the stars because of holes worn through the ceiling, windows to replace broken ones. It only touched the outer core of the islanders' many needs, yet they were euphoric, and eager to speculate on what other good fortune might come their way while their landlord was in such a generous mood.

Laura tried to be happy for them, but suspicion kept her happiness in check. She was certain Barnaby hadn't thought of all this on his own; after all, he'd been satisfied with the status quo for years now. Which meant Garret must have taken Barnaby's request for counsel to heart and was advising him on what to do to make a better impression on the investors. Why? He didn't strike her as the type of person to do something for nothing. What was he planning to get out of all this?

The sound of an approaching vehicle made her glance up and pause at the turn leading down to her clinic. It was Barnaby's Jeep, but someone else was driving. Seconds later she recognized the classically handsome man from the helicopter.

As he pulled to a stop blocking her path, he smiled, deepening the lines that bracketed his mouth. "Good morning. The psychic, I presume?"

Would every word out of his mouth sound as though he was quoting Shakespeare? she wondered, taking in his powder-blue shirt and white slacks. Amusement lit the amber lights in her eyes. "Let me guess," she murmured, tilting her head. "The pirate's first mate."

Laughter sparkled in his own eyes, which were the color of the most coveted jade. "I was warned the association might condemn me, but I come on a mission of mercy, madam. Your services are needed at Whitehall."

Laura frowned slightly. "What's wrong?"

"O'Keefe's not himself."

"I would think that cause for celebration, not concern."

"He's been rubbing at his leg all morning."

She sighed and glanced at the house, torn between her responsibility as a doctor and her instincts for self-preservation. "You know, Mr.—"

"Channing." He extended his hand. "Giles Channing, at your service, Doctor."

"Mr. Channing, I'd prefer your candor," Laura said, giving him her hand.

"Call me Giles and it's yours."

"Is he really not feeling well, or is this simply a trick of his to get me over there? I should warn you, I don't take it lightly when I discover I'm being manipulated."

Giles pursed his lips and whistled softly. "Barnaby was right about you two. Makes me wonder what I've missed."

"Meaning?"

He tugged at his earlobe and gave her a smile brimming with boyish appeal. "If you don't mind, I'd like to start this conversation over again. I think I'd prefer having your friendship to being on your hit list."

She had to admire a person who knew when to quit. "I know someone who could take a lesson or two from you," she murmured.

Giles didn't pretend to misunderstand. "It might help you understand him better if you knew he's more used to having to worry about what a woman wants from him, than worrying how to make one take him seriously."

"Sorry. I'm fresh out of violins this morning."

"Even if I told you he really doesn't look well?" Seeing the betraying flicker of concern in her eyes, he pressed onward. "It's obvious he hasn't been sleeping and his appetite wouldn't keep a man half his size alive for long."

Laura studied him silently, wondering how far she could trust this man who owed his allegiance to O'Keefe. Yet she knew in the end it wouldn't matter; she was a doctor and if O'Keefe needed her services, she had to take care of him.

"One question. Did he ask you to come get me?"

"When I jumped into the Jeep, he was swearing up a storm."

"That's all I needed to hear." She climbed in beside him. "Let's go."

From the porch, Garret watched their approach, his eyes narrowing, his temper heating. He cared for Giles; he respected his business acumen and his ability to focus on details. He was amused by the Englishman's romantic escapades, which—as far as he was concerned—made far more interesting copy for the paparazzi than his own.

But he was damned if he was going to sit back and watch while his friend made a move on Laura.

What had he said to get her into the Jeep with him? he wondered as they drew closer. What was she saying that was making him laugh like that? By the time they pulled up in front of Whitehall, jealousy was clawing at him and it took an enormous effort to sit quietly and wait.

"Laura, dear," Barnaby said, as both he and Garret stood to greet her. "It's about time you paid us a visit."

"I've been busy. Sit," she urged them, though she only looked at Barnaby.

"You work too hard."

Someone had to, she thought, suppressing a rush of annoyance. Things weren't going to improve simply by willing it. "I decided to reestablish those swimming lessons I used to give after the little Pierre boy almost drowned last week."

"Ah, yes. I heard about that. Tragic situation that would have been." He turned toward Garret. "Ironic, isn't it? We live on an island, yet until Laura came and started giving lessons, few here knew how to do more than paddle around in the water. We owe you so much, my dear."

"You can start paying me back by telling me you've been behaving yourself," Laura said, glad for the opportunity to change the subject.

"Haven't had a choice. You know when you give Sarah instructions, she follows them religiously. But forget about that." He gestured expansively. "Tell me what you think of the place."

She caught the eavesdropping gardener's anxious look and forced herself to smile. "I've never seen it looking better—the cottages, too. George and Miss Jewel asked me to thank you again for their new screen door. She says she doesn't know what she's going to do with all her free time now that she doesn't have to chase flies and lizards out of the house."

"Glad to be of help, but—er, it was really O'Keefe's idea."

For the first time, Laura turned completely toward Garret, though she'd been aware of him and that he'd been watching her from the moment she arrived. As their gazes locked, she felt the connection, an electrical jolt that made the skin at the back of her neck prickle.

She could see for herself that Giles had been right; Garret hadn't been sleeping or eating well. But it would take a lot more than a few restless nights and a few pounds to dim his compelling presence.

"I'm told your leg's been giving you problems."

Garret watched her exchange her medical bag from the right hand to the left, the only indication he had that she might not be as calm as she seemed. But it was a crumb he was grateful for. Inside, his own nerves were in chaos. If only he'd never given in to the impulse to touch her, kiss her, he might be able to leave and forget. Yet the memory of her softness was burning ever deeper in his mind and he only had to close his eyes to remember her sweet-wild taste. She was only a woman—worse, a woman who scorned what he was—but she was the woman he wanted. He had to make that crumb mean something.

"My doctor told me I had to be patient," he replied, suppressing the temper his jealousy spawned. "I'm trying."

She had to drop her eyes to his gray-and-yellow striped linen shirt to hide the effect his quiet voice had on her. "And your ribs?"

"They're better."

She gestured to his half-eaten breakfast. "So much better that you've lost your appetite? Given up sleeping?" She inclined her head toward the front door. "I think we'd better go inside and I'll see for myself."

"Need any help?" Giles asked cheerfully as he leaned against a porch pillar, watching.

As he stood, Garret shot him a look of warning. "Thank you, but I think you've done more than enough already."

Minutes later, when Laura had shut the door of his bedroom, she turned to Garret and watched him sit down at the foot of the bed and mechanically go through the motions of unbuttoning his shirt. "What's going on here?" she demanded, not for a moment believing this exhibition of passivity. "I'm warning you, O'Keefe, if Giles lied and this is just a trick—"

"Lied?" Garret paused on the last button. "What did he say to you?"

"He asked me to come look at you. He was concerned about your health."

"I thought—" He shook his head deciding to leave well enough alone.

"You thought *what*?" she asked, moving closer. The evasion in his eyes, the look of guilt, was fleeting but she saw it and exhaled on a growl. "You men make me sick. I am not some *trophy* you can compete for."

"You call him Giles and me O'Keefe."

"*He* hasn't abused my trust yet."

"For God's sake, Laura, how was I to know you've been hurt before?" Too late, he realized what he'd said. As realization set in she turned on her heel and headed for the door. He grabbed her wrist.

She turned on him, seething. "You and Barnaby have been discussing me. He told you what I'd shared in confidence during my interview for this job," she whispered, closing her eyes against tears of humiliation.

"I asked," Garret replied, gently correcting her. "Because I didn't understand you. And I wanted to try. Laura, I'm sorry for that, but there's something between us, something that refused to let me go."

"Lust."

"Oh, yes." He stroked the inside of her wrist with his thumb. "There's that—and more. You're different from the other women I've known."

"As a novelty, poverty wears thin faster than the finish on costume jewelry," she said, refusing to be seduced. She couldn't afford to make a mistake again. Why couldn't he accept that and leave her alone?

"I need to prove to you I'm different, too," he said, as if reading her mind. "Or maybe I need to prove it to myself. We all have ghosts, Doc."

Every instinct inside her screamed for her to get out now while she could. It would be dangerous to begin understanding him, wondering about his past, what he was really like. If she left him packaged in a stereotype, she could go on with her life. It might not be fair to him, but she was dealing with survival here and she could still count; three strikes and you were out. She was a lot of things, but suicidal wasn't one of them. She told herself that as she put down her bag and dropped to her knees beside him.

"Don't tell me about your ghosts, O'Keefe," she muttered, rolling up the cuff of his white shorts one more time in order to remove his bandage. "I don't want to hear about them. I don't want to be your friend or anything else. Just let me do my job here and leave."

Softly spoken words, and meant with no rancor, yet they sliced into him, made him grip the bedspread with both hands. "Can you? Is it going to be that easy now that we both know what the other tastes like, what happens when our bodies touch? Are you going to try to dismiss me like a troublesome dream?"

"I'm going to give it my best shot."

What saved him from doing something drastic was feeling her fingers tremble against his thigh. He looked down and saw her draw her hand away, flex it before returning to her work.

Another crumb, he thought, slowly releasing his pent-up breath. Somehow he would collect them all and make a banquet out of them.

Whether anyone was ready or not, the investors arrived, and then the night of Barnaby's dinner party. No one looked forward to the evening less than Laura.

It had been a long time since she'd dressed for a formal dinner party, a long time since she'd dressed for any event at all. As she stood before her dresser mirror and tried to brush out the result of forty minutes of her curling iron's work, she was tempted to forget the whole thing. Spending an evening with Garret was going to be hard enough on her nerves. She didn't need the added pressure of making small talk with Barnaby's three new guests who were—as far as she was concerned—a threat to Big Salt's future.

But if you don't go, who'll look out for the interests of the islanders?

"Low blow," she muttered to the woman in the mirror.

And awful hair.

"I give up." She tossed the brush onto the dresser and reached for an elasticized band and a handful of bobby pins.

Several minutes later there was a knock at the door to her apartment. She dropped the second pearl stud earring she was about to clip to her ear. Now who could that be? she wondered, hoping it wasn't a patient. She was already running late. Maybe Mo had forgotten something earlier.

But it wasn't Mo; it was Garret. He filled the doorway as only he could, resplendent in a white dinner jacket, black tie and slacks. He didn't resemble a pirate tonight, or a god, but what he was—a very rich man with abundant power. All she could do was stand there and stare at him.

"Why the devil don't you lock your front door? Do you realize anyone could simply walk in here?"

His annoyance released her gratefully from her hypnotic state. "*Anyone* did," she snapped back.

What had he expected? he wondered, amusement replacing his concern for her safety. Chances were if some drifter or lowlife had snuck in looking for something to steal, she would face him down with a skillet in one hand and a scalpel in the other. The satisfying image allowed him to relax one shoulder against the doorjamb and take a more thorough survey of the woman before him.

Beautiful.... He'd told himself she wasn't, but he'd been wrong. She possessed a quiet, understated beauty that needed no makeup or jewelry to enhance it, and she

knew exactly how to show it to its full advantage. Her
gown was jade-green silk, the style oriental. Though de-
murely cut, it fit her body like a caressing hand, and he
experienced a flash of jealousy at the thought of sharing
this vision with anyone else.

"I came to give you a ride," he murmured, his gaze
slowly returning to her face.

"It wasn't necessary. I could have walked."

He glanced down at her delicate high-heeled sandals
before giving her a crooked smile. "In that case..." He
lifted a hand to caress her left ear. "I came to tell you
you're missing an earring."

Laura remembered the dropped pearl and, flashing
him a disgruntled look, went to hunt it down. It gave
Garret the opportunity to admire the graceful curve of
her neck, accentuated by the way she'd drawn her hair
into a sophisticated coil at her nape. But his mouth went
dry as he noticed the side slit in her gown that offered a
provocative glimpse of trim ankle, shapely calf, and while
retrieving her recalcitrant earring, sleek thigh.

"All right, I'm ready," Laura said, after giving a final look in the mirror and grabbing up her black evening bag. But as she approached him, she found he
wasn't in any hurry to budge. "Are we going or aren't
we?"

"If I tell you how lovely you look, will you stop snap-
ping at me like a bad-tempered terrier?"

"I—thank you." She took a deep, steadying breath. "I
suppose I'm slightly nervous about tonight. Where's your
cane?"

"In the Jeep. I'm needing it less and less," he said, as
he moved aside for her to pass him. "Laura, I wanted to
talk to you about those men."

Outside the sun was setting, turning the sky shades of tangerine and gold. The scent of wildflowers saturated the sea-damp air creating an intoxicating atmosphere that made Laura almost forget where she was going and why.

"They haven't already tried to persuade Barnaby to sell, have they?"

"No. It doesn't work that way. Besides, they still don't believe my reason for being here and they're cautiously trying to find out if they'll have to bid against me." He assisted her into the Jeep and braced her in with his arms. "I just wanted to warn you to be careful. They're a smooth bunch and you're a unique experience for them."

Despite the warm breeze coming off the ocean, Laura felt a cool prickle against her bare arms. "A 'unique experience'?"

"Laura, you're a beautiful, intelligent woman, but you're out of your depth when it comes to dealing with men like—"

"You?" Her fingers itched to slap him and she closed them more firmly around her bag to quell the impulse. But her eyes spoke volumes. "Don't worry, O'Keefe. I've learned how not to throw myself at wealthy men, just as I've learned not to slurp my soup."

He ran a hand over his hair. "That's not what I meant."

"Could we please go now?"

"Damn it, will you listen to me?"

"Then I'll walk," she said, trying to push him aside so she could get out.

Garret stayed put. "You have to be the most infuriating, stubborn woman I've ever met. I'd like to—" He caught a glimpse of the time on his watch and swore softly. Late. They were late, and if he didn't get them back up to the house, Giles was going to come looking for them. Collecting himself, he stepped back and matched her glare for glare. "Stay where you are or by heaven I'll tie you in."

He'd planned a tender wooing; he ended up acting like an insensitive jerk. He'd meant only to shield her from a type of man he was all too familiar with; instead, he'd behaved just like them. Garret wondered if he could sink any deeper into the well of depression he'd dug for himself.

As the evening progressed, he watched Laura handle herself with the grace and charm of a woman who'd been raised to do little else—and discovered he could.

"Mr. Van Damm, I've read you have an intriguing hobby—raising orchids, isn't it?" Laura said conversationally to the silver-haired man who was seated on her right during dinner. "Unusual for a man from your part of the world, isn't it?"

"Not at all. Did you know that there are some species that can only be found in Alaska and the Himalayas?" He leaned toward her, warming to his subject. "My newest fascination is with miniatures. I have an exquisite *oncidium pusillum* that is currently thriving in a snail shell."

"You must get Barnaby to have someone take you to the waterfall on the south side of the island where the children like to play. There's a yellow variety I think you might find interesting, though I haven't a clue what species it is."

"Marvelous. I shall."

"Dr. Connell, you must indulge us in the pleasure of giving you a tour of our yacht before we leave."

Laura turned, forcing herself to meet the dark, enigmatic eyes of the Saudi who sat on Garret's left. "That would be lovely, Mr. Safar,'' she replied, her smile purposely cool. "But I have a consultation on Abaco tomorrow and I'm afraid I won't be back before you leave."

"How unfortunate. Perhaps another time."

Garret frowned, wanting to know if it was only the aversion he sensed she had to Safar that encouraged her to find an excuse to decline. "I hope none of your patients is seriously ill," he offered solicitously.

Laura took a careful sip of her wine before directing a frigid look his way. "One of my patients is dying, Mr. O'Keefe. He waited too long before coming to see me because pride wouldn't allow him to accept medical care without having the money to pay for it. Now I'm reduced to searching for a way to make his final weeks as comfortable as possible."

Even at the head of the table, the lively conversation among Barnaby, Giles, and the third guest of honor, an American, dwindled to an uncomfortable chuckle.

"Well." Barnaby adjusted his glasses before tossing his napkin on the table. "I don't know about you, but I feel like a stuffed pheasant. Coffee and brandy in the study, everyone?"

Laura didn't know how he managed it, but somehow Giles was beside her chair casually announcing he wanted a smoke first. He invited her to join him for a quick stroll around the garden out back. She gave him a smile in gratitude and, slipping her arm through his, allowed herself to be escorted outside.

"I don't know how to thank you," she murmured, stopping beside a flame-colored hibiscus.

"Forget it." He leaned back against the trunk of a gnarled old tree and reached for one of his thin cigars. "We all have our moments."

"I certainly picked mine." Sighing, she tilted back her head and looked up at the stars crowding the sky. "It's no excuse for embarrassing Garret, but I kept listening to all that talk about money, and power, and possessions.... None of it means a thing against the value of a human life. Can't they see that? And then Garret made that token remark. He didn't care. He was just jealous because I'd been ignoring him all evening."

"I don't doubt that he was, but you're wrong about him not caring." Waiting for her to take that in, Giles studied her over the red-tipped end of his cigar. "Do you know when I first met that blue-eyed madman, he was climbing a high-voltage utility tower in California to rescue an eight-year-old boy who'd chosen a dandy way to show his friends he was as tough as they were. There I was, an earl with no earldom trying to explore beyond the thirteen colonies—"

"You're an earl?"

"Well, actually I'm second in line. The point is O'Keefe's Jaguar was blocking my way to Xanadu and we ended up working together to get the boy down. Most people would have given the kid a good tongue-lashing and left it at that, but he took a genuine interest in him. The boy was from a broken home, a potential drop out from society, and O'Keefe got him the help he needed to put his life and his mother's back on track."

Laura strolled over to inspect a bed of roses. "That's commendable, but I don't think I need to remind you you're talking about the same man who ousted over a dozen families from a New York apartment building because he wanted to replace it with a glitzy high rise."

"Mmm. I remember that one. So does he. Why do you think he takes these long voyages out here, testing the elements, testing himself? He was born with everything anyone could ever want. He didn't need to worry about a career or pension. But he decided at an early age that he wanted to work, *needed* to work, to prove himself. The only problem is that like many of us, he's found the prescribed route often isn't enough to assuage the guilt of being born rich *and* talented."

"Are you telling me about him or you?"

Giles grinned wickedly. "He's wealthier."

"You're the worst flirt."

"So he tells me." He tossed away his cigar and held out his arms. "Come here and give us a hug. Then we'll go back inside and tell them all to go to hell if you like."

Laughing softly, Laura let him embrace her. It was nice being in his arms. Though tall, he wasn't as big as Garret and she didn't feel that wild, almost reckless, need she felt when Garret held her. She felt peace. The only problem was she didn't need Giles to feel anything but friendship for her.

"Don't look now but we have company." Giles kissed her on the forehead and placed her at arm's distance. "Much as I wouldn't mind slaying dragons for you, love, this is one battle I think you're better off handling on your own."

Silhouetted at the back door, Garret watched the tender scene and felt a curtain of red cloud his vision. As Giles approached him, he curled his fingers into his palms, trying to remember that ten years of friendship should count for something.

"Is she all right?" he asked with more control than he thought himself capable of.

"No," his friend replied amiably. "But she'll scratch your eyes out if you try to tell her otherwise. Fascinating lady. Too bad you saw her first."

Garret didn't return his smile. "Try to remember that."

Giving him a slight bow, Giles maneuvered around him and went inside. Laura approached cautiously.

"I'd like to apologize for taking out my anger on you," she began quietly. "I was rude."

"You don't have to go back in there if you don't want to."

"I won't. If you'll tell Barnaby I had an emergency at the clinic—"

"Let me walk you home."

She shook her head. "That's not a good idea."

"Why not?"

"Because you wouldn't leave it at that," she replied honestly. As he reached for her, Laura stepped back. "No, Garret. Please don't take advantage of my weakness for you."

"Ignoring this isn't going to make it go away."

"Then leave!"

"I can't." He reached out and pulled her into his arms. "I won't."

He kissed her, hating her for finding the core in him that was vulnerable, wanting her as he'd never dreamed of wanting. Disregarding pain, he molded her to him; forgetting there were others nearby, he abandoned himself to need. There was no sweetness in this kiss, only spice. She would understand and concede. In his mind, in that fever that blinded him to all else, that was the only feasible solution.

"Garret." His name was a breathless moan whispered into his mouth. He claimed that, too, as he claimed her, everything, in his not-quite-civilized need to possess. She was tempted to let him. She was tempted to let this golden-haired giant conquer the barriers of her defenses and satisfy the yearning he'd started. The wanting was a restless viper writhing within her, urging her to melt against him and take all that he offered.

But what would be left? As fear shimmied its way into her consciousness, she trembled against him. What would be left when, after she gave everything, it was time for him to leave?

"Garret . . . I can't," she whispered, sliding her hands up to his shoulders, to frame his face, asking for understanding.

He made a sound, a growl of denial he uttered against the sensitive side of her throat.

She bit back a whimper and closed her fingers into his beard. "Garret . . . no," she whispered, pushing at his head with all her might.

He dragged air into his lungs and crushed his lips against her right palm. "Laura, for the love of heaven—"

"But it's not heaven you'd leave me with." She wrenched herself out of his arms. "Go away," she begged. "Please, just leave me alone!"

Slipping off her sandals she ran, a frantic Pandora who'd caught a glimpse of the demons she'd released. Garret watched until she was one with the night. The totality of the darkness she left him in was no larger, no blacker than the abyss he felt engulf his soul.

Seven

"The glover's suture has the needle passing through the loop of the preceding stitch, Mo. And watch your spacing. It's too wide."

The young man glanced up from the chicken he was practicing on and gave her a frustrated look. "You think this bird cares? Anyway, I'm never going to get it right, Doc."

"You'd be surprised. With enough practice there isn't a couture house in Paris that wouldn't snatch you up as a seamstress."

"Thanks a lot."

Hearing the yearning in his voice, Laura sighed and gave his shoulder a squeeze. Then she went to lock her supply closet. "Since we can't refreeze it, why don't you go deliver that poor bird to Gina with our compliments. It's about time for you to meet the children down at the beach, anyway."

That cheered him somewhat. "I'm glad you let me take over those swimming lessons. At least seeing that the little ones learn something makes me feel useful."

"You *are* useful and not only to them, but to me. Don't you ever forget that. Now get out of here. If you need me for anything, I'll be up at Lizzy's. The baby developed a nasty case of colic and Lizzy has the new-mother jitters."

Mo glanced at her from beneath his dark, curling lashes. "Are you going to stop by and see Mr. Barnaby? Sarah says he's been real depressed since those investment people left."

Laura made a pretense of checking her medical bag to see if she needed to restock anything in it. She had a good idea why Barnaby was depressed; Giles had told her the news the day before when he'd come by to say goodbye before departing to take care of business for Garret.

The investors, it seemed, had indeed made Barnaby an offer, but it wasn't to build the luxury hotel on the far side of the island she'd heard rumors about. Oh, they wanted to build the hotel all right, but on the ground where Whitehall was standing. It was the better location, they'd insisted. The supply of springwater would be more easily accessible. Of course, Barnaby would have to move, and the farming, such as it was, would have to make way for tennis courts, a golf course, and naturally a pool. One mustn't forget that not everyone enjoyed swimming in saltwater, they'd reminded him. They said they felt fairly certain that most of the islanders could be employed in one capacity or another; however, since Barnaby would be handsomely compensated, that was all that mattered in the end, wasn't it?

Now everyone was waiting on pins and needles to see what Barnaby would decide. She knew this was a blow to him. He'd always assumed that no matter what became of Big Salt, he would be allowed to spend the rest of his life in the house he'd been born in; and she was genuinely concerned what this might do to his health. But she was having difficulty summoning sympathy for him. If he decided to sell there were going to be many others who were going to need it more.

"I don't know," she said at last. If she went over to Whitehall, chances were she would also run into Garret, and *there* was another confrontation she wanted to avoid. "It all depends on how the afternoon goes."

Hours later, Laura stood on the northern point of the island overlooking the sheerest drop to the sea and took a deep breath of the tangy ocean air. The breeze was light, yet gently tugged at the strands of hair that had worked themselves free of her braid during the afternoon. Behind her she heard the soulful spirituals sung by the workers in the cane fields, and farther away offering a dubious accompaniment to the music was the droning of the diesel engine that operated the cane press.

She liked to come here at the end of a particularly stressful day, watch the sea gulls dive for food, and listen to the music of nature blend with that of man. The symphony of the earth working was how she thought of it. As long as it continued, she could. It gave her a sense of stability, and hope.

But she wasn't there more than a few minutes before she heard the sound of the Jeep coming up behind her. Barnaby, she thought. He'd come either to ask for her counsel or forgiveness. She straightened her shoulders but didn't turn around. Either way she would take this news calmly, she told herself. Besides, maybe she was worrying for nothing. Maybe he'd decided to turn down the offer.

"Laura?" Garret stepped out of the Jeep and, as she spun around, he extended his arm to stop her. "No, don't leave. I didn't come here to bother you."

"Then why did you come?" Her tone was cool despite the way her heartbeat had accelerated at the sight of him. He wore a navy shirt and jeans, workman's clothes that emphasized the muscles of his shoulders and thighs. His hair was windblown and his face had lighter streaks at his eyes indicating he'd been out in the sun for several hours. He looked like the man she'd first believed him to be, and she didn't like what that did to her defenses.

Ignoring her question, he glanced over her shoulder to consider the view. "Nice place, isn't it? Looking out from here reminds me of the feeling I get when I stand at the bow of a ship. Just me and all that space. It's almost spiritual."

Laura turned back to the ocean, not wanting to be seduced, only to catch herself seeing it through his eyes. She wrapped her arms around her waist. "Say what you came to say, O'Keefe."

He lifted his right leg and rested it on the running board of the Jeep, then ran his hand along his thigh. It was feeling stronger ever day, and yesterday he'd removed the bandages from around his ribs. They weren't completely healed yet, but they soon would be, and that would take care of his flimsy excuse for remaining here. He wondered if Laura would feel any real regret if he told her he was contemplating chartering another boat and leaving. Probably not. All her thoughts and energies were focused on this poor doomed island and its hapless inhabitants. But even as he admired her commitment, he resented it.

She looked as tired as the shirt and khaki slacks cling-
ing to her body. How long did she think she could continue being the nurturing center for this place? How long
before exhaustion or bitterness took its toll on her? She
was generous and she was strong, but she was kidding
herself if she thought that was enough.

What a temptation it was to live up to his reputation,
be the pirate they accused him of being. He would like to
snatch her up one night and carry her off to sea with him.
He almost had himself convinced he could do it without
compunction, too. There he might have a chance to reason with her. There he would unleash the passionate
woman he knew she kept carefully hidden from the rest
of the world. He could give her a life she'd never known,
dress her in silks, and shower her with pearls children
brought up from the sea in their hands. There wasn't
much he would deny her if only she asked.

And they would enjoy each other, he was certain.

But he was more certain that she would jump ship at
the first port and run back to this place, for the fact remained: he might want her, but here she was needed. For
a woman like Laura that was far more persuasive. Sighing inwardly, he brought his daydreaming back under
control.

"I came to ask you to come help me with Barnaby.
He's over at the shed. I suppose I better tell you now that
he's been drinking."

"You've been here long enough to know that's nothing new," she replied, determined that this time she
wouldn't give in so easily.

"Heavier than usual."

She took a deep breath and massaged her aching
shoulders. "What's he doing there in the first place?

When he's usually ready to tie one on, he closes himself in his study.''

"He wanted to 'survey his kingdom' as he puts it. I knew if he got behind the steering wheel of that Jeep he'd probably drive himself over a cliff, so I told him I'd take him wherever he wanted to go. But he's starting to make the men at the cane shed nervous. I've tried to talk him into going back to the house, and short of knocking him over the head, I'm out of ideas. I thought you might have one.''

"None that sounds as good as yours." But seeing her sarcasm was wasted on him, she gave a weary shrug and picked up her medical bag. "Oh, all right. I'll see what I can—"

Before she could finish, there was a horrible scream from the shed, followed by frantic shouts. Barely exchanging more than a glance with Garret, Laura raced around to the passenger's side of the Jeep, while he climbed in his side and started it up. They covered the short distance in less than a minute, but by then there was a good-size crowd gathering around the shed.

Laura didn't wait for the Jeep to come to a halt, but leaped out and pushed her way through the curious onlookers, steeling herself for the worst as she listened to the screams of the man in the throes of some terrible pain. But when she entered the inner circle of the group, she saw things were worse than she could have imagined and her stomach lurched in reaction.

It was Shrimp's father. Somehow his right arm had become mangled in the bull gears of the cane press. "For God's sake," she cried, pushing her bag into someone's arms, "get him out of there."

"Trying," one of the men muttered, as he struggled with a punch and hammer in an attempt to remove the key from the hub of the gear. "But dis be one old and rusty machine. Not gonna give easy."

A second man was doing his best to keep Caleb calm while supporting his weight. "Only thing to do is run him through. He'll bleed to death before we get dat drive gear off."

Garret joined the inner circle and quickly surveyed the situation. "He's right, Laura."

"Are you mad?" she asked, shaking off the hand he laid on her shoulder. "Then he's sure to lose his arm."

"What's more important, an arm or a life?"

Would he be so quick with his glib reply if it was his arm that was caught between the gears? Laura took one look at Caleb and swallowed the angry question, knowing they didn't have the time to waste on worthless supposition.

She reached for her bag. "At least let me give him a shot of morphine before you do anything else."

She worked quickly, but was aware of all the eyes watching her, especially those of the man she was trying to save. Caleb had a wife and three other children besides Shrimp. He was as strong as a bull, and a good provider for his family; but there was fear in his pain-glazed eyes now. Only a year or so younger than Laura, he was not yet ready to face death.

"It's going to be all right," she whispered, administering the shot. "In a few moments you won't feel a thing."

"Ah, Caleb... I'm sorry," Barnaby mumbled behind her. "I'm so sorry."

Laura shot him an angry glance over her shoulder. "Be quiet! Better yet go home."

Unaware she'd even spoken he continued. "It's all my fault. I shouldn't have been speaking to you. I d-didn't know you were standing so close...."

Laura turned on him, her eyes narrowing. "What did you say?"

Barnaby was almost too drunk to stand and wobbled precariously as he struggled to focus on her. In his hands was his hat, crushed against his chest. His face was ruddy and webbed with broken blood vessels, souvenirs from countless other binges; his eyes were bloodshot, and haunted by the horror of what he knew his intrusion had caused.

"Laura...don't look at me that way. P-please. I'll pay his medical expenses. I'll—"

"His *expenses*?" Suddenly something snapped inside her. She grabbed him by the front of his shirt and shook him as if he were no more than a rag doll. "Damn you— Do you know what you've done? Have you any idea?"

"Laura." Garret grasped her by the shoulders to draw her back. "Easy."

"Let me go!" With fury to spare for both men, she jerked free from his grasp and turned back to Barnaby.

"You promised to *do* something with this island," she ground out, her voice shaking. "You promised these people a decent life. But look at them. Look at *him*!" She pointed toward Caleb. "Primitive equipment, inferior housing...this whole place is decaying just like you are. You're nothing but a useless drunk. You might as well sell out to those *sharks* for all the good you're doing us here."

The rest of her tirade was obliterated by the sound of the diesel engine starting up again. Before she could do little more than turn around, it was over. Caleb, gratefully drugged, was being lowered to the ground.

Laura used whatever was available to create a tourniquet to slow the bleeding, then directed two of his friends to carry him to the Jeep. Finally she turned back to Barnaby. "Get someone to give you a ride back to the house on one of the carts and radio for the medical helicopter."

He began to shake his head and nearly toppled over. "I don't—I don't think I'm in any condition."

"You listen to me," she shot back, her look lethal. "You *get* yourself in condition. I don't care what you have to do, but you sober up and make that call. Now move!"

They took Caleb to her clinic. The island grapevine had already reached Mo and he was there. Caleb's wife came running as they were carrying him inside. Laura only had to look at Garret and he took control of the situation, drawing the woman back as she tried to follow into the examining room. Already forgetting them, Laura went to work.

It was quiet when she reemerged from that back room, and as she expected, Shrimp was now there along with his brother and sisters. Their frightened expressions made her summon the most reassuring smile she could.

"He's lost a lot of blood but he's stabilized. Now let's hope the helicopter gets here."

It seemed to take an eternity. But when they heard that welcome shout from someone keeping watch outside, Laura directed the men to once again carry Caleb back to the Jeep and they slowly made their way up to the landing site. There they transferred him over to the care of paramedics. His wife climbed aboard with him, but Laura had to snatch back Shrimp who wanted to go, too.

As the helicopter lifted off and flew away, a great white egret turned salmon pink by the descending sun, peace settled once more over the island. At last the soft sounds of Shrimp's weeping sister could be focused on. Laura sank to her knees and gathered all the children close, assuring them that the time for tears was over; their father would be back and soon. Mo volunteered to see they got home and a neighbor came forward to help, assuring Laura she would stay with them until their mother returned.

Slowly, the crowd that had gathered dispersed. As she watched, Laura felt the effects of the stress-filled afternoon finally hit her, and she slumped wearily against the bumper of the Jeep. Several yards away stood Barnaby. He'd worked at cleaning himself up since leaving the cane shed, and though he still looked terrible, it was clear he was far more sober. It was also impossible to miss that he was a shattered man.

As he began to turn away to head back to Whitehall, Laura called to him. She was no less angry than she had been before, but she wasn't proud of the violent instincts she'd experienced back in that shed.

She met him halfway. "Are you all right?"

He dropped his head in shame. "Don't waste your concern on me. I don't deserve it."

"I'm inclined to agree with you, but I'm still a doctor and you look like hell."

"It's only fair, I would think," he replied, giving her a sad smile. "Go home, Laura. You've done well today, but a magician you're not."

Watching him walk away, she combed back loose tendrils of hair from her face. Her stomach turned queasy as she caught the lingering scent of disinfectant soap on her hands, and she was reminded that it had been hours since she'd eaten. But she knew it would be hours more before she would be able to keep anything down. Right now all she wanted was a hot shower and the oblivion of sleep. Just as she wondered if she had the energy to walk back to the clinic, Garret appeared at her side.

"I'm driving you home."

He spoke quietly, but there was no mistaking the look in his eyes or the hold he had on her arm. She could go with grace or with a fuss, but go she would. Too tired to do more than cock her left eyebrow, Laura allowed herself to be escorted to the Jeep.

They made the trip in silence, each involved with separate thoughts, separate worries. The salmons and tangerines of sunset were giving way to dusk, wrapping them in a cocoon of mauve and gray. It should have been a time for whispers and reflection, a time for relaxation. But the tension remained. Grew.

Even before Garret came to a stop before the entrance of the clinic, Laura was reaching for her medical bag. Belatedly she remembered she hadn't needed to bring it with her on this trip. Feeling like a fool, she uttered a brisk "Thanks" and dragged herself out of the Jeep.

She was barely inside the white picket fence when she heard him kill the engine. Her pace faltered momentarily. No, she thought, not now. Tomorrow she would deal with him, argue with him, whatever it would take, but not tonight. She was running on emotional empty, a hairline away from doing something stupid. Couldn't he understand that?

By the time she reached her front door he was directly behind her. She spun around and stretched her arm to block his path. "Go away."

"Not a chance."

She closed her eyes and summoned what little control she had left. "I appreciate what you did today. I'll even take back some of the things I said about you. But make it tomorrow. Right now I'm tired, sweaty, and I'd really like to get out of these bloody clothes."

"You also need a stiff drink."

"First thing on my agenda."

"I could use one, too."

Impulse tempted her to slam the front door and if his hand or foot got bruised in the process, all the better. But conscience made her hesitate, and in that hesitation she found herself backing up into the reception room of her clinic.

Not liking any better the feeling that gave her, she turned on her heel and swept through the reception room. Under the force of her entrance, the door to her apartment bounced off the back wall.

If he insisted on staying she would ignore him, she told herself, heading straight for the pantry where she kept her meager liquor supply. She slammed the bottle of brandy onto the counter and reached up into the open cabinet for two unmatching glasses. Those, too, hit the counter with a velocity that should have shattered them. She poured an eyebrow-raising portion of brandy into one glass, and, taking it with her headed for the bathroom. "Lock the front door on your way out," she said without turning around.

She closed the bathroom door with slightly less force and slumped back against it. Fine job, she saluted herself in the vanity mirror. She was turning into a first class— Her gaze dropped to her clothes.

The sight of blood was something all medical students had to adjust to early in their careers, and like everyone else, Laura had her memories of that initiation that could be as embarrassing as they were traumatic. But for the most part they remained exactly that—memories. Yet every once in a while, it came back—that first revulsion, that first dread of having it *touch* you, mark you as the one responsible, the one who should make things right, the one who had failed.

Laura downed a good portion of her brandy in one overambitious swallow. Within seconds her vision was blurring and flames were burning a path to her stomach. As she reached for the counter to steady herself, she knocked the glass out of her hand. It toppled into the sink and shattered.

A shattered glass, a shattered life . . .

The shaking started subtly. She felt it like the first tremors of an earthquake. The tears came more slowly— or maybe because she felt numb, it took a while to feel them running down her face.

Fear seized her, the panic of losing control. In a desperate attempt to stave off complete hysteria, she ripped off her clothes and wrenched at the shower taps until water pounded against tile full force. As the first sob built in her throat, she stepped under the punishing spray hoping it would muffle the sound.

On the other side of the bathroom door Garret listened, gripping both sides of the doorjamb. He'd been listening since he'd heard the glass break. It provoked him into gulping down his own brandy. But just as concern had led him to where he now stood, indecision kept him from going in.

She wouldn't thank him for intruding.

But she could have cut herself on the glass.

Maybe not. He could already hear the shower being turned on.

What about her other wounds, the internal ones?

He leaned his forehead against the door. Who was he to help there? She was right about him; he could wheel and deal; he understood money and the power it had over people. But when it came to knowing what else made people tick, he was lost. He'd rarely allowed himself to get close enough to anyone to learn, rarely trusted. His world was one of polite strangers, competitors facing him across boardroom tables. What did she need? He didn't know where to begin guessing, and she was in no condition for clumsy handling.

Then he heard the racking sobs. They scraped at him, dull claws that made him ache in a way no amount of brandy would ease. Even as he reached for the doorknob, he was wrestling with the buttons on his shirt.

She didn't hear him enter; she didn't feel his presence until he stepped into the shower stall. Spinning around, she stared through her tears and the steam—shock and humiliation quickly giving way to fury.

"Get out. How dare you—get *out*!"

As she struck at him, he grabbed at her wrists, but in her excited condition she was more than a handful. "Laura, stop it. I only want to help."

"I don't want your help."

He might as well have been wrestling with a wildcat. "Damn it. I don't want to hurt you!"

"Then get out! I don't want you here."

Wrapping one arm around her waist, he locked her body to his. It trapped her left hand between them and she struck at his shoulder with her right one. In self-defense he clamped his free hand around her wrist, completely immobilizing her.

She swore, then wept harder in frustration.

"I hate you," she sobbed, finally dropping her head against his shoulder. "I hate y-you."

"I heard you the first time." Gulping air, he lowered his head to hers. Drenched, her hair still carried the scent from her last shampoo. He closed his eyes and let her cry.

It lasted forever... until the water no longer burned but soothed... until the pounding spray became a massage... until he became aware that she was no longer pushing at him, but curling into his embrace. Until he became aware that it felt too good having her against him this way.

He took a deep breath, released her hand to stroke her hair, and thought of liquid silk. Giving in to impulse, he kissed the top of her head.

"Better?"

She hesitated before answering. "Why couldn't you just leave?"

"I heard the glass break."

"It didn't touch me."

"Then I heard you crying."

It seemed the most natural thing to continue stroking her. Her neck and shoulder muscles were knotted with tension and he massaged her gently to relax them. A washcloth and soap were within reaching distance and he wet both, rubbed them together, creating an overflow of soapsuds, a pink meringue that dripped from his fingers. When he smoothed it over her shoulder and down her back, he felt her stiffen, then heard her reluctant sigh of pleasure.

"Feel good?"

A heavy dollop of soap gave up its resistance to gravity and slid down between her breasts, sensitizing each inch of skin it caressed. She became unbearably aware of the way her breasts were beginning to throb, the way her nipples thrust against his hair-matted chest in undeniable arousal, the way her body was beginning to heat to a melting point. She felt his desire become a point of physical evidence.

"You have to stop."

"Sooner or later. Maybe later," he murmured, sliding his hands down over the subtle swell of her hips. She was so slender she seemed fragile, and yet, like the willow, he knew she was stronger than she looked.

She bit her lower lip as he gently urged her hips against his. Just as lightly, she pressed her palms against his chest to place a whisper of space between them. "I don't want this," she moaned.

He gazed into her somber brown eyes, red and a little glassy from crying, then kissed them closed. "Don't want what?" he asked, taking advantage of the small distance between them to slide the soapy washcloth along her right collarbone, her left. Lower.

"This . . . touching. Seducing."

"Is it unpleasant?"

"You know it isn't. But I—" As he slid the backs of his fingers over her left breast, stroked the underside with his fingertips, her nerve endings experienced a series of short circuits leaving a tingling that centered at the pulse points of her body. Her breath caught. Her mouth turned dry, and she licked droplets of water from her lips to ease it.

"You what?" Fascinated with the depth of her reaction, he did it again, this time lingering to trace his thumb around her nipple. She would taste like wild honey and cream, he thought, his own mouth going dry.

"O'Keefe . . . it won't change anything."

He banked a sudden rush of anger, but his grip tightened. "Just once do something because you *want* to, Laura. Need to."

She closed her eyes and shook her head. "I don't want to want you."

"But you do, don't you?" Once again he drew her close, but as he felt himself sheathed by the warm, satin smoothness of her thighs, his control slipped a notch. He combed his hands into her hair to hold her still and kissed the corner of her mouth, her delicate cheekbone, sipped water from the tip of her chin and nipped at her parted lips. "Don't you?" he demanded, burning with a craving he knew only she could satisfy. Still she resisted him and his next kiss was a little more insistent.

"Yes." It was no more than a whisper, but it said everything. She was through with fighting him or herself.

Hands that had tried to push him away reached for him; lips that had fought to remain unresponsive now sought passion. It had been so long since she'd wanted, felt wanted, that the flood of emotions spiraling through her left her dizzy, yet intent, weak, yet demanding. Needing more, she dropped the last barrier of her defenses and offered him everything.

Colors. He'd never thought of desire being a thing of colors and yet behind his closed eyelids he saw them. Violets. Blue-whites. Silver so brilliant it blinded. Edging closer to the source, he backed her to the tile wall. Then he remembered where they were and what limits his condition put on the situation.

Uttering something closer to a growl than a groan, he turned off the water.

"Garret..."

He quickly framed her face with his hands and claimed her mouth for a kiss that made her immediately seek another. Instead, he caressed her swollen lips with his thumb. "In bed. It will be better there."

Helpless not to, Laura followed.

Eight

Their hearts pounding, they stepped into the unknown, quiet as the darkening room they entered. A light breeze drifted in from the opened windows. It carried the scent of rain. The cooler air skimmed over their wet skin offering a blissful, if minute, relief from the fever that burned just below the surface. They hadn't bothered with towels, they didn't hide their feelings; drawing together for another overwhelming kiss, they sank onto the bed.

Their sighs blended like their tastes, creating something original, unique. They explored each other with the unrestraint of longtime lovers, but the excitement of discovery was new, heady. They didn't speak, but when they gazed deeply into each others eyes, the communication was there.

More. Anything. Everything.

Garret thought he could spend a week simply kissing her. Again and again he returned to lose himself in her wild, sweet taste, and he knew he could drive himself mad thinking of anyone else touching her. Even now the thought came to torment him and his touch became less gentle.

His eyes burned with possession as he slid his hand down her body from throat to knee. Her skin shimmered with droplets of water, and the supine grace of her body made him think of sirens and shipwrecks. Had he known she was here, would he purposely have risked navigating the reefs that stormy night in order to reach Big Salt? As she gently pushed him onto his back and began placing tiny nibbling kisses down his chest, his wondering ceased. He stopped thinking at all.

It thrilled her to touch him. He was so strong, yet beneath her lips she could feel his heartbeat thrum as erratically as hers. Never again would she be able to touch him with dispassion, without remembering how the muscles on his shoulders and arms seemed to coil, harden under the lightest stroking of her fingertips; how his breathing became shallow when she placed moist, gentle kisses over his bruised ribs. Physically, financially, he might be the most powerful man she'd ever known; but here, with her, he was vulnerable. It made her feel strong, and as she slid her lips over the scar on his thigh, she conceded that it made her feel very generous.

Tonight was hers. Theirs. From the first time their eyes had met they'd known this was coming. Maybe she'd known even before. What was behind them she couldn't help. What lay before didn't matter. Just this once, as he'd urged her, she wanted to forget everything and simply feel.

She rose over him and, braced by her arms, lowered herself until her breasts brushed against his chest. Watching him, she swayed one way and then another, following a rhythm more instinctive than planned. She caught her breath at the slight bite of his fingers at her hips, and then sighed as they trailed upward to cover her breasts.

She'd been right; his hands did make her feel small, but oh, how precious. As his thumbs circled her beaded nipples, a current of pleasure raced through her, prickling her skin like hundreds of tiny lovebites.

Her voice no more than a breathy whisper, she asked for more. "Taste me."

Muttering something unintelligible, Garret rolled her beneath him and, lowering his mouth to her breast, gave them both what they wanted. He thought he could temper the hunger; she arched off the bed and demanded more. Never had there been anything like this. He was burning up and it wasn't enough. She was making him desperate.

Her name was a groan on his lips; the appeal glittered almost as a warning in his pale eyes. He slid completely over her asking, *demanding* that she understand.

She reached up to caress his beard, slid her fingers deep into his hair, and drew him toward her. "Yes, I know."

He kissed her with the same swiftness that he claimed her body with, a primitive need driving him to take what was his. *His.* Did he say it? He believed it. Suddenly. Completely. Buried in her, surrounded by her, caught in the whirlwind essence of her, she was his and he took her with a force that in the last sane corner of his mind he knew should have frightened her. But the power of her passion matched his. Groaning, he took them to a deeper, darker place. Laughing, she rushed him onward. Together they plunged into an abyss and were reborn.

Outside, the wind picked up, bouncing the bamboo shades against the windows as it swept inside. A heavy drop of rain tapped against the roof, followed by a few more, then a torrent opened upon them. Keeping her eyes closed, Laura took a deep breath of the fresh air, then exhaled. It was all she had the energy to do.

Minutes passed, or perhaps it was only seconds. She stretched a little, enjoying the strong, cool breeze that swept over her damp and flushed body. She knew she could easily drift off to sleep and decided that until she did, she would be content to feel. But the one thing she refused to do was think.

Beside her, it was all Garret *could* do.

What had happened just now? he wondered, feeling the smoke begin to clear. What the hell had happened? Cautious, he raised his hand to inspect it, half expecting to see ashes instead of healthy flesh on bone. Still, there *was* a faint unsteadiness to it. A small price for surviving a fiery cataclysm.

He turned his head to look at Laura in time to see her open her eyes and stare up at the whitewashed ceiling. "Are you all right?" he whispered gruffly.

She didn't look at him, nor did she reply. With an inarticulate oath, Garret combed both hands through his hair, then raised himself on one elbow.

"Laura, if I hurt you—"

"No."

"But you're so small."

"Not really. It's just that it's been a long time for me."

The flat tone to her responses wasn't enough for him. He leaned forward and brushed the tip of his tongue over her right nipple, more satisfied with her gasp and the faint shiver he felt race through her. "I'm glad," he replied. "But I still should have been more gentle."

"No, I—" Embarrassed for what she'd been about to say, she looked away.

Garret curled his hand around her jaw and turned her back to face him. "I liked it, too, you little fool," he muttered, then kissed her soundly. Within seconds the passion was back as if it had never been satisfied. It was like wildfire, threatening to quickly slip out of control and consume.

Only the need for oxygen forced Garret to end it. He rolled onto his back and, gulping air, covered his eyes with his forearm.

"Well, we've done it now," Laura murmured, trying for a light touch.

He went very still. "Utter one word of regret and I swear I'll strangle you with my bare hands."

"No. I won't be a coward about it. But—oh, God, O'Keefe," she half whispered, half moaned, as the serrated edge of desire's ache seesawed through her. "I don't know if I'm ready for this."

"We'll take it one step at a time. That's what my college French tutor used to tell me."

"How did you do?"

"Not worth a damn."

She didn't think she would laugh again for days, but she did and, hearing her, Garret gathered her into his arms so that she lay half sprawled across his chest.

"Be careful," she warned, trying to brace herself on her arms. "I don't want to hurt you."

"Hurt me, just don't leave me."

The gruff tenderness in his voice touched her as nothing else could and she stopped resisting to gaze down at the man holding her. O'Keefe. She'd just made love with the pirate himself, she thought. It had been fierce and wild, and as wonderful as anything she could have expected. But this gentle side of him, this tenderness that slipped out when he entreated, needed, worked its way under her defenses even faster.

"You can't be real," she whispered, stroking the beard that had stroked her.

This time he glanced away, but only for a moment. "I warned you before not to complicate it. I'm simply a man, Laura."

"Not a simple man."

"I'm the man who wants you more than he's ever wanted anyone, anything in his life."

She shook her head because it was too tempting to believe and eased herself off the bed. "You know what? I'm thirsty. Hungry, too. Why don't I get us something? Brandy, cheese, and fruit, I think. The cheese is made from our own goat's milk, but it's an acquirable taste. I'll be right back."

Garret watched her retreat to the bathroom. Shortly afterward she came out dressed in the short black kimono-style robe he'd noticed hanging behind the bathroom door and headed for the kitchen. She briskly went to work pulling out a tray from one cabinet, a knife from a drawer, food from the refrigerator. She didn't turn on a light but relied on the beam arrowing in from the bathroom, and she didn't stop talking. From the age of the brandy she repoured, she went on to debate the quality of this year's mango crop, to the problem of keeping crackers from going stale in their humid environment. It was nothing short of nonsense—and slowly, Garret began to relax.

She was afraid. Along with comprehension, he felt a surge of compassion for her. She expected him to dress and walk out of her house, out of her life the way her father did to her mother...the way her fiancé did to her. It was simply her way of trying to protect herself from being hurt again and, even as he found it frustrating, he understood.

He wished he had some magic words to say to her to make it better, easier, but none came because he knew she was right to be wary. He still wasn't sure he believed in what he was feeling himself. But if she needed him to give her a little space to get her bearings, a while to get acclimated to the idea of their being lovers, he could play along.

As she carried the tray to the bed and placed it between them, he sat up and dragged a few pillows from the headboard for them to rest on. "Well, that looks like almost enough for me. Where's yours?"

She laughed, though it sounded suspiciously more like relief than amusement and gave in to the impulse to feed him a cracker with cheese. "You'll share or I'll banish you from this dry haven and you can ride back to Whitehall in that waterlogged Jeep."

He accepted the glass of brandy she handed him and smiled, approving of the sparkle returning to her eyes. "Hmm... I've had my fill of feeling like a drowned rat. At any rate, it would be a shame to water down such a fine brandy."

Feeling the tension easing between them, Laura picked up her own brandy and sipped, silently toasting herself. She was doing the right thing, she told herself. Two ships that pass in the night and all that. They'd both been through a rough day; they were emotionally vulnerable. It only followed that their lovemaking would seem particularly poignant. It was safer, saner to let things cool down.

"Is it a fine brandy?" she asked, honestly not knowing. Not being particularly fond of alcohol, she'd never paid much attention. The bottle had simply been in one of her supply boxes several months ago and this was only the second time she'd opened it.

"It's perfectly suited to your goat's cheese."

This time her laughter came more easily. "No wonder Barnaby let me have it."

Garret watched her even, white teeth bite cleanly into a slice of mango, her tongue dart out to lick away the juice from her lips. Tempted to do that for her, he reached for another cracker. "It was good of you to go as easy on him as you did after the helicopter left."

She shook her head, dismissing it the same way she wanted to forget about the day. "I don't want to talk about Barnaby tonight. Tell me about you. Tell me where you go when you shed your power-broker's mantle and sail off in your boat."

"My former boat," he amended dryly.

"You'll get another."

He shot her a quick glance, wondering if she knew looking into that was one of the errands he'd charged Giles with. "Most of the time I have a destination picked out, somewhere I've heard about, someplace I want to explore, something I've never done and want to do."

"You're easily bored."

"I prefer to think of it as needing challenges."

"Is the glass half empty or half full?"

He gave a teasing tug to the sash of her robe. "I should know better than to split hairs with a doctor."

She shifted to a more comfortable position and her robe slipped open, exposing one creamy shoulder. "What about this time? You make it sound like this time was different."

This time he'd been suffocating to the point where he couldn't concentrate, couldn't make any sense out of what he was doing, let alone why he was doing it. This time he'd been running, not exploring. He didn't want to be reminded of that.

"I suppose this time I just wanted to see how fast *Thetis* could go."

And maybe how far? "I suppose for some people the world is shrinking faster than it is for others."

He concentrated on swirling the brandy that was left in his glass. "Let me know when it's my turn to analyze you."

Temporarily forgetting about consequences, Laura reached out to touch his hand. "I wasn't being critical."

"What then?"

"I was only thinking it must be hard to always be needing fresh challenges in order to feel life has any purpose. After a while I guess you run out of places to look."

He picked up her hand and lifted it to his lips. "Maybe I've been looking in the wrong places."

She began to speak but nothing came out. With just a look, he wiped out everything but her memory of what it felt like to be in his arms. Feeling the attraction heating again, she cleared her throat and gently extricated herself from his grasp. "Maybe we'd better change the subject."

"What's safe?"

"Tell me how you got that scar on your cheek."

"You'll be disappointed. I didn't earn it in a duel, but falling off my father's polo pony. I was ten. It also earned me a sound whipping for disobeying his orders not to ride him in the first place. Fortunately *that* didn't leave any scars."

"I wouldn't be so sure about that," she murmured, hearing the edge of bitterness in his voice.

"You're analyzing again."

Ignoring him, she gave in to curiosity. "Why didn't the two of you get along?"

Garret polished off another cracker and slice of fruit before answering. When he did he kept his voice low, his tone apathetic. "He was the most competitive man I've ever known. He never wanted a son. He wanted a clone he could test himself against."

"Competition isn't unnatural between fathers and sons."

"Is that so? Then you'll find this story fascinating. For my fifteenth birthday his gift to me was a woman. Do you need me to clarify that?"

"I didn't mean—"

"He had her waiting for me in my bedroom when I came upstairs from the dinner party he'd thrown in my honor. She told me we had an hour. Only later did I discover that he'd bought himself the rest of the night with her."

"Oh, Garret." She had to look away from the bitterness she saw in his eyes. "Your mother—she wasn't alive, was she?"

"No, and I suppose you could say it was to his credit that he waited until he was between wives before he pulled that. He had three more after my mother died. None lasted more than a few years, which should give you a vague idea of the depth of feeling involved. The last was the youngest, the prettiest, the one I believed he cared for the most. I paid him back with her." He gulped down the last of his brandy. "I thought I would feel retribution; instead I felt dirty."

Laura remained silent, not knowing what to say. It would be an overstatement to say she was stunned—in her line of work it was unwise to think one had heard everything—but she was aggrieved to learn he could seek revenge so cruelly.

"I told you we all have our ghosts," he muttered, lashing out at the panic he felt simply watching her.

"So you did. Would you like more brandy?" she murmured, reaching for his glass.

Before she could take it and the tray, he all but dropped it on the floor beside the bed. Ignoring the resulting clatter, he swept her into his arms, canceling any thought she might have had of escape by straddling his left leg over both of hers.

"Look at me, damn it. If you're angry, disappointed, say it."

"Your past is your business."

"I never said I was a saint."

"I don't recall comparing you to one."

But he wanted her respect. More, he needed her trust. He reached up to touch her cheek and groped for the right words. "Laura, I'm not an easy man. Hell, most of the time I don't even care if I'm a nice man. I was raised to be an achiever and I've succeeded; my net worth is twice what my inheritance was, and you don't do that by turning the other cheek. But I *am* honest," he added more quietly, "and when I tell you that you're under my skin, it's not a line. So tell me to stay or tell me to go, but if I stay... I'm through talking. The past has nothing to do with this."

Maybe talking was their mistake in the first place, she thought, feeling the white-hot heat flaring in his eyes melting down the walls of her resistance. They were from two different worlds; their lives went in two different directions. But tonight, in this, they were compatible. As she slid her hands up his chest and around his broad shoulders, she decided it was enough.

"Stay," she whispered, drawing him down to brush her lips against his. "You were right before. I don't need to be alone tonight, and I don't want to be."

Relief came like a flood and his hold tightened. Ignoring the pain he inflicted on himself, he strained to get closer yet. "Now kiss me the way you want me," he demanded, his look triumphant, possessive.

Without hesitation, Laura pressed her mouth to his and the storm broke once more. Where did this need for such passion come from? She was a quiet, logical woman, yet he stripped her of her ability to do or want anything except to lose herself in the delirium of his lovemaking. She was losing her mind—or was it her heart? As his breath brushed across her cheek and he ran his lips down her throat, she shivered and inched closer. That would make things all the more dangerous. He could hurt her; ultimately he would leave her. But she couldn't stop. When he returned to her mouth for yet another kiss, she was waiting and matched his demands with her own.

Their hands reached simultaneously to untie the knot in her sash. When they only succeeded in tightening it, Garret growled with impatience.

"Why did you bother with this in the first place?" he grumbled, pausing momentarily to scowl down at her waist.

"I thought it would stop you—us—from doing this again."

Something wicked and not quite civilized flared in his eyes. His chest rose and fell with each rapid breath. "Well, you're wrong," he replied. Without blinking, he reached beneath her and dragged the robe off her shoulders. Silk ripped and her breath caught as he bared her to his appreciative gaze.

"You—*pirate!*" she cried, half laughing.

"Aye, lassie," he replied in a throaty brogue, bending to run his lips down over her smooth, taut stomach. "And the pirate's a hungry man."

But a pirate, Garret reminded himself, conquered and plundered. He was in control and followed no lead nor law but his own. Yet as Laura wrapped herself around him and urged him on, he heard gates slam, bolts lock, then smoke and fire rise and consume...and he couldn't help but wonder—who was plundering whom?

Nine

The first thing Laura discovered when she woke the next morning was that she was alone. Her next conscious thought was that maybe it was a blessing. She felt awful. When she dragged herself out of bed and stumbled to the bathroom to face herself in the vanity mirror, she decided she didn't look much better. Her eyes were still red from crying, and her hair—hair that she never did get around to drying—looked like something she'd seen in a magazine article about New Wave styles. Granted, she had a certain glow, but closer inspection revealed *that* was nothing more than a whisker burn.

In the shower she bemoaned the soreness of muscles and joints she hadn't known she possessed. She scrubbed herself mercilessly with a natural sponge, and if—when she emerged a few minutes later—she still felt as though she'd been dragged against her will through a marathon race, at least she didn't feel as if she'd finished on her hands and knees. Though not enthusiastic about it, she was prepared to face the day. But only one thought came to mind.

Where was Garret?

When she went to make herself a cup of instant coffee, she found her answer in the note stuck inside the coffee tin.

Knew you'd make your way here eventually. See you before you miss me. Garret.

Her lips twitched in amusement. The man had a sense of humor, but he still didn't know a thing about her.

She *already* missed him. She'd missed him the moment she opened her eyes and realized she was alone in bed with nothing to keep her company except her own thoughts—and doubts.

"Don't start making this into something it's not," she told herself a while later when she added boiling water to the heaping teaspoon of crystallized flakes in her mug. What had happened last night was a singular experience, and it would *never* have happened if she'd been thinking clearly.

But then again it *had* happened and it was wonderful; and, *yes,* she wanted to believe he meant what he said in that note. She wanted him to come back to her.

You're asking for trouble.

He'd made her feel special, beautiful.

That European princess he'd been photographed with at Cannes was beautiful; you're a seven and a half on a good day.

Eight. Besides, anyone would look good in a tiara.

"Ow!" she cried, as she scalded her tongue on the hot coffee. She set down the mug, thoroughly disgusted with herself.

If she didn't pull herself together, she was going to go crazy or injure herself. Since it was clear the situation was temporarily out of her hands, it would be foolish to do either. If and when he came back, she would deal with her feelings then. Besides, she reminded herself, what if he *had* been here when she woke? What would she have said to him? As she ran her sore tongue against the inside of her lower lip, her frown grew more troubled. Things could have grown extremely awkward after "good morning." Unless they'd abandoned the need for talking at all.

She covered her face with her hands and groaned. That did it. It was time to get dressed and go to work. She had a clinic to run. She adjusted the towel she'd wrapped around her hair and went to get dressed. Pulling out a clean shirt from the dresser drawer, she turned her thoughts to less complicated matters.

"Well, Elias, how does it feel?" Laura asked as she tossed the arm cast she'd just removed into the trash bin. "It probably could have stayed on a few more days, but as long as you promise not to do any climbing for a while, you should be all right."

"I'll be careful, Doc." He peeled bits of dried plaster from his skin and tested the arm's flexibility. "Kinda stiff."

"That's normal. Give it a few days to loosen up. But if you have any lingering pain, I want you to come see me right away."

"Don't plan on needing to, Doc," he said, as she indicated he could scrub off the remaining plaster at her sink.

She patted him on the back. "That's the right attitude. Put me out of business."

When he was finished, she walked him out through the reception room and at the front door reminded him to tell Gina hello for her. "And no wrestling with the children!" she called as an afterthought.

Behind her, Mo cleared off his desk and chuckled. "You're in a better mood than I expected."

Laura shoved her hands into the pockets of her khaki slacks and gave him a dry glance. "Yeah? Mind over matter. I decided things could have turned out a lot worse."

"Amen to that. By the way, Shrimp came by. He wanted you to know his momma just got home and she says Caleb's doing fine. They're going to keep him for observation another few days. He should be released early next week."

"That's great. Maybe I'll go up to see her later on. I would imagine right now she's trying to catch up on lost sleep." She glanced at her watch and saw that it was barely eleven. "Short day for us. Are you hungry?"

"Not really. Anyway, I thought if you didn't need me, I'd take off and catch a ride to Hooper Island."

Laura didn't have to ask why. One of the residents, a pretty girl of seventeen, had been brought to her last week suffering from a jellyfish sting. Mo had been thoughtful and a bit restless ever since. She couldn't blame him. The girl seemed sweet and just as taken with him. Something like this was bound to happen sooner or later, she thought philosophically. It was only his zealous desire to be a doctor that had kept him from noticing there was indeed more to life than studying.

"You should've told me earlier. I could have managed on my own today." She glanced at her watch again. "You'd better hurry. Doesn't the trade boat usually leave around this time?" When he admitted it did, she all but pushed him out the door telling him to have a good time. "Just don't forget to come back!" she called after him.

She watched as he ran down the road leading to the beach and then raced along the dock to where islanders were still loading crates of fruit and vegetables on board the sturdy boat. Later tonight it would return and tomorrow the dock would be crowded with islanders collecting their share of whatever their crops had yielded in trade.

"Doc, you busy?"

Laura turned to see Lizzy coming down the dirt road. "Not at all. Where's the baby?"

"Home wid momma. Mr. Barnaby sent word there'd be no working today."

"I hadn't heard that." She was surprised and pleased. She thought he would still be locked away in his rooms sleeping off the effects of his latest binge. "Well, I hope you're here to visit and not because you're feeling ill. Would you like to come in and have some iced tea or juice?"

"I can't stay. Momma thinks I'm looking for our goat. It ate through its rope again and wandered off." As Lizzy joined Laura on the front steps, she gave her a quizzical look. "What happened to you, Doc?"

Laura self-consciously covered the right side of her face. "I—um, guess those natural sponges are too rough for my skin. Come inside and tell me what I can do for you."

The younger woman followed her into the reception room, but paused there, suddenly looking embarrassed. "You're gonna be mad. Momma's already fussing up a storm."

Laura sat down on the edge of Mo's desk, comprehension coming quickly. "Joe's back."

"He came back from Abaco last night. He's got a steady job now," she said proudly. "And he seemed real pleased wid de babe. He's gonna marry me—just as soon as he gets a little money together."

"Get it in writing."

Lizzy gave her a desperate look. "Doc, I'm crazy 'bout de man."

It wasn't news to Laura, and she rubbed at the space between her eyebrows, knowing she could talk until she was hoarse and it wouldn't change a thing. She'd seen this situation happen again and again. For every responsible family man like Caleb there were two like Joe who took off at the first sight of their girlfriend's swollen stomach.

"What is it that you want me to do? You don't expect me to plead his case with your mother, do you?" she asked, remembering the usually calm woman's temper.

"I want you to give me something to—" She ducked her head in embarrassment. "I don' want no more babies right now."

"Have you lost your mind?" Laura's own temper flared. "You're still in no condition to even be *thinking* about that."

"But I will be soon and I need to be smart dis time."

"Smart would be to tell that no good—" Seeing the petite woman's shoulders begin to droop, Laura held up her hand. "I'm sorry. You're right. I have no business meddling in your private life."

"I know you mean well, Doc."

"Unfortunately good intentions are about as useful as rainbows."

"What?"

"Wait here." Laura went back into the examination room and returned in less than a minute. "Here," she

muttered, taking Lizzy's hand and pressing a small
packet into her palm. "If he comes within five miles of
you, give it to him."

The young woman took one look and handed it back
to Laura. "He won't use it."

"Why not?"

Lizzy struggled to explain, but before she could barely
begin, the sound of a woman calling her made her jump
nervously. "That's Momma. I gotta go."

"Wait a minute."

"I'll come back tomorrow. I promise," she insisted,
seeing Laura's look of doubt.

Watching her run out, Laura slumped back against the
desk, feeling helpless and more than a little frustrated.
She hadn't handled that one well at all. The trouble was
she was fairly certain that no matter what approach she
used, the result would have been the same.

She stood up, drawing her hand out of her pocket.
Poor Lizzy, she thought. She really picked a winner in
Joe. What was his problem with this, anyway? Anyone
with two ounces of common sense would understand—

"Oh, God," she whispered, staring down at her palm.
"Oh, my God."

Stunned, she walked out her front door oblivious to
the bright sunshine and the gull that playfully swooped
low over her head.

Just when he thought he'd looked everywhere and a
strange sense of unease was beginning to gnaw at his insides, he spotted her at the far end of the beach near the
place he'd been told he washed ashore. Crab Cove or
something like that. He'd gone back once out of curiosity, the way some people did to their places of birth because they thought they should look different, special.

Naturally they didn't, and neither did Crab Cove—until he saw Laura sitting there on a huge mound of rock that made him think the place should more aptly have been called Tortoise Cove.

Even from this distance, he could see that she was daydreaming as she sat staring out to sea. He wondered if she was thinking of him. He'd had a full, hectic day, and yet throughout it, she'd been in the forefront of his mind, as strong as a physical presence. It was pleasant, but it was no longer enough. Shifting into first gear, he cut a hard left turn and drove toward her.

When she heard the Jeep, he saw her turn her head and he had to smile at the way she quietly watched him. Would he ever tire of the way those gentle, doelike eyes observed him so seriously?

He brought the Jeep to a halt a few yards away from her perch and, resting his forearms on the steering wheel, grinned up at her. "Looking for victims?"

"Business is always slow in good weather."

"If I offer to drive this thing into the surf, would I do?"

Her smile came more easily than she expected it would and, rising, she eased herself down the rock. Dozens of questions buzzed unanswered in her head, but all she could think was how good it felt that he'd kept his word and had come. She took in his half-unbuttoned white shirt and shorts, so striking against his dark tan, his golden hair and beard that competed with the sun in brilliance. He looked gorgeous—and invincible. How could she think she could ever resist him?

By the time she reached the sand he was out of the Jeep, watching her in that intent way that tempted her to run those last few steps and throw herself into his arms. Her heart, its beat already accelerated, started to hammer crazily. When she was within arm's reach, he drew her close until she was able to feel his heart against her breast, and discovered that it, too, was far from steady.

"Miss me?" he drawled.

"A little."

He narrowed his eyes, unsatisfied, then lowered his head to crush his mouth to hers. The tentative, lighter mood between them was instantly replaced with something far more intemperate as he thrust his tongue deep to conquer anew what he'd repeatedly claimed for himself last night. But again, as she met him halfway, he found himself tangled in her taste, seduced by her softness, and imprisoned by her passion.

A heartbeat away from giving into base instincts, he framed her face between his hands and broke the kiss. Resting his forehead against hers, he tried to slow his rapid breathing. "Confess," he rasped, "before you have me on my knees."

Her laughter was no steadier than his voice. But then she surprised him by wrapping her arms around his neck and, uttering a shaky moan, burying her face against him.

Bemused, he tentatively stroked her hair, then her shoulder, before protectively drawing her closer. "Hey, what is this?"

"Nothing."

Concentrating only on her, Garret frowned. "It doesn't feel like nothing to me."

"All right, it's not 'nothing'. It's everything."

"You see? That clears things considerably."

"I don't expect you to understand, but you don't have to make jokes about it."

Thoroughly confused, he gently disengaged her arms so he could see her face. "I have a feeling you started this conversation before I got here." It was then he saw the reddened skin along her jawline and cheek. Murmuring his apology, because he knew only too well how the abrasion had happened, he touched his lips to the tender spot. "All right," he sighed, more than willing to start over again. "I'm sorry for making jokes, but what else can I do when I don't even know what *it* is?" Then a look of comprehension lit his face. "You're not telling me you didn't find my note this morning?"

"I found it." Telling herself she was acting foolishly, she drew back another step, hoping the distance would make her think more clearly. She brushed at wisps of hair tickling her face and she gave him a self-deprecating smile. "Forget it. I'm just a bit strung out, that's all."

"Hard morning?" he asked, taking her hand to make it impossible for her to retreat further.

"Something like that." As he raised her hand to his lips and began placing soft kisses across the back of each finger, she pulled free and shoved both hands into her pockets. "Please don't do that. I can't think straight when you're nibbling on me as if I were an hors d'oeuvre."

"Why do you have to think at all?" he replied, drawing her back into his arms and kissing her forehead, the tip of her nose, and then her chin. "Why not just kiss me the way you did a minute ago."

Before she could even think to refuse, he again closed his mouth over hers, holding her there by placing his right hand at the back of her head. This time the kiss was more tender, promising, yearning. She felt her heart swell with emotion and curled her fingers into tight fists, trying to keep some corner of her mind lucid.

"I missed you. I want you," he whispered, scattering desperate kisses over her face. "Here. Now. With the sun bright and the sea close. Even when I was getting up to leave you this morning, when I thought it impossible after what we'd shared through the night, I wanted you.''

''Garret—''

''Make love with me.''

''This isn't a private beach.''

''Then let's go somewhere that *is* private.'' He edged backward, taking her with him, ready to carry her into the Jeep if necessary. She lost her balance and, stumbling, she jerked her hands out of her pockets to brace herself against him. Something sharp poked him in his chest and he uttered a colorful imprecation.

Closing his hand over her own, he stared down at what was trapped between their fingers. Laura watched his eyes widen, his eyebrows lift before he gave her a look that was rife with incredulous laughter.

''Does this mean yes?''

Ten, even five, years earlier Laura would have nearly died of embarrassment, but now that she was older and more shockproof, she briskly pulled her hand free and calmly slipped the packet back into her pocket. ''Don't be crass.''

''You mean one honest response doesn't deserve another?''

More than disappointed that the tender moment between them had been destroyed, she was angry at his attitude. ''If I were a man, I think I would slug you right now.''

''Sweetheart, if you were a man, we wouldn't be having this conversation. Now would you mind telling me what's going on here?''

She bent over to adjust the strap that had slipped on her sandal. ''I was simply trying to help a patient. That's all.''

"Oh. *Oh*." He tugged at his right earlobe and gave her a crooked smile. "You threw me for a minute because I know last night we didn't—"

If she wasn't still tempted to take a swing at him, Laura would have laughed as she watched his expression change when the full impact of what he was about to say finally registered. "No, we didn't, did we?" she said with saccharine sweetness.

"Wait a minute," he began, not really certain how to respond, but sure that he didn't care for the way she was glaring at him. If there had been a slipup, he wasn't the only one who'd made it. "You're the doctor!"

That did it, Laura thought. She turned on her heel and started walking away from him. No, she wasn't going to stand there and listen to that. Did he think she needed him to remind her? What did he think she'd been doing these past few hours if not mentally kicking herself black-and-blue? No one knew better than she did about the risks they'd taken last night.

Behind her, Garret stood, finding himself in one of those situations where he wished he could turn back time. Had he ever said anything so insensitive, so stupid in his life? Besides, no one could ever accuse him of putting the burden of responsibility on someone else; he couldn't afford the risk. Last night should have been no different. But last night he'd lost his head.

Laura was more than halfway down the beach when she heard the Jeep start up. Knowing there was no way she could outdistance him on foot, she took a shortcut through a palm tree grove. Even so, Garret beat her.

He was parked at her front gate, leaning against the spare tire as she crossed the dirt road and, without preamble, he picked up where they'd left off. "I didn't mean to say that."

"Yes, you did."

When she tried to pass him, he caught her arm. "Laura, let me apologize and then we'll talk."

"If we talk, there'll be trouble. I'm in a fighting mood, O'Keefe. Now let go."

Instead he swept her into his arms. Ignoring her indignant cry and furious attempts to free herself, he began limping up the walkway.

"Are you crazy? Put me down!"

"In a minute."

"You're going to reinjure yourself."

"And here I was worried you no longer cared. Get the door will you, sweetheart?"

She did, but only to end this ridiculousness, and *only* after shooting him a venomous look. He didn't put her down in the reception room as she'd expected, nor did he release her after he'd kicked the door to her apartment closed. When she realized where he was headed, she decided he was pushing his luck.

"Don't even think it," she said tightly. A moment later she found herself stretched horizontally across the bed with his big body pressing her deeply into the soft bedding. Angry tears began to blur her vision as she wrestled to free her wrists from his grasp. "Damn you, O'Keefe."

"We really have to work on this unpleasing habit you have of swearing at me."

"I'd like to do more than swear at you."

"Shh." He kissed her left cheek and, as she jerked away, her right. When she did it again, he focused on the side of her neck and then the frantic pulse beat at the base of her throat. He'd carried the scent of her soap on his body all day and now he found it again on her. It gave him a strange sense of intimacy, of homecoming, and he forgot that he'd only meant to soothe her temper so that she would listen to him.

He trailed his kisses downward. At the first button of her shirt, he paused, trying to nudge it undone. But the material was stretched too tightly. He released her right wrist so he could unbutton that first button, then the next one and the next. Her undershirt made him smile.

"I don't want to sleep with you," she ground out, using her new freedom to push at his shoulder. But already she could feel her body betraying her, heating and tensing in anticipation of where he would touch her next.

"I don't want to sleep with you, either," he murmured, nudging her shirt out of the way with his nose. "At least not yet."

He nuzzled her breast through the cotton, wetting her shirt and she felt a betraying shudder of desire move through her. If he'd been as he was last night, all passion and fierce need, she would have found the strength to resist, but now his touch was careful. His concentration was no less focused, but there was a tenderness in his caresses. Even in the hand that gripped her wrist there was caution as he stroked his thumb against her stretched tendons. And hadn't he told her himself he wasn't a gentle man?

"Please," she cried, making a last attempt to reason with him. "This only complicates things more."

"No, it doesn't." He turned his head to award the same thorough ministrations to her other breast. "It clarifies them."

Laura shook her head, knowing she should disagree, but the reasons grew vague in the mists of her growing arousal. She felt him slide down her T-shirt. Then his attack on her senses became more ardent and she felt the last of her anger dissolve. It was no use, she realized. She couldn't fight him. Worse, she couldn't fight herself.

Feeling the change in her, Garret released his hold and slid up to kiss her. Gently. She whimpered and drew him closer, her body already beginning that fine trembling he was coming to know. Her vulnerability to him filled him with as much wonder as it thrilled him. He would apologize again, he thought fleetingly. Later. But first he would show her that if he couldn't always understand her, he cared enough to want to try. Women were such complicated creatures, and this one most of all.

As she drew her hands down his back and began pulling his shirt free from the waistband of his shorts, he murmured his approval against her lips. He wanted her hands, but not simply for this moment. That realization was swift and sure. He wanted *her*, but for more than today. And he would have her, he promised himself reaching for her belt.

Slowly, carefully, he undressed her, treating her clothes as if they came from Rodeo Drive rather than the mail-order catalog. If he understood nothing else about her, he understood this: she knew what it was to do without loving as much as he did. In that respect they were two of a kind. Knowing his own emptiness, he sought to fill hers.

He was far less patient with his own clothing. The sight of her lying there, her long lashes half-lowered over eyes dreamy with desire for him, made his blood heat too quickly. But he did take time to reach over into the pocket of her slacks. When she drew him down against her, they both felt the shudder that coursed through him. But even as he slipped into her, it was with a restraint that surprised him and enchanted her.

It almost hurt, so sweet was their slow joining. Their gazes locked, they reached for each other's hands, seeking and finding mutual understanding.

He whispered her name. The word held a promise and an entreaty. With a kiss they made both come true.

They were quiet for a long time afterward, both wondering about the things they wanted, needed to say, both reluctant to break this peace they knew couldn't last. Garret rolled onto his back and drew her to his side. Lifting her braid, already half undone, he finished unbraiding it. As he slowly combed his fingers through it, he admired the lush feel and rich color.

"Beautiful. Like mink in firelight," he murmured.

"It's very thick. I'm often tempted to cut it short. But then I remember how my mother used to love to brush it and I can't do it."

He tried to picture her as a child. She would have been all legs and huge eyes. He wanted to know about those days. He wanted to know everything about her. But there were so many other things they needed to deal with first.

"Laura, I want to take care of you."

Giving up on the notion of taking a catnap, she opened her eyes and gave him a faint smile. What a sweet way for him to put it; perhaps she'd been hasty in losing her temper with him. "You don't have to get noble on me. I've been trying to count and I'm sure there's nothing to worry about."

"That's not what I meant."

Laura lifted her head from his shoulder to give him a doubtful look. "It's not?"

"Wait a minute. That didn't come out right, either." Since when, he wondered, did he have a problem with making himself clear? Raising himself on his elbow, he reached out to tuck her hair back behind her ear. "*Yes, I* meant that. Of course, I did. But I also meant more. We're good together, Laura.''

Suddenly realizing what he meant, she dropped her gaze to the blue-and-green-print bedspread. ''You don't have to say anything more. You want us to continue seeing each other until you leave. All right,'' she agreed, lifting her chin. ''But I don't need you to take care of me. If we're going to have an affair, we'll do it as equals.''

''It would please me to do something for you,'' he murmured, leaning forward to brush his lips over her shoulder. ''Give you something you wouldn't get for yourself.''

She shook her head. ''I'll be your lover, but not your mistress. When you walk out of my life, I don't want to feel as though I've been duly compensated.''

''What if I'm in no hurry to walk out of your life?'' he asked, with a slow, sly grin.

Her heart made a wild leap behind her breast, but she ignored it. ''I'll still feel the same way.''

''No, you don't understand.'' He sat up completely and reached for her hand, his excitement growing. ''I have news. I should have told you before. It's the reason I've been gone all day. Barnaby isn't going to sell the island to those investors.''

With a joyous laugh, she threw herself into his arms and began smothering him with kisses. ''Oh, that's wonderful. I was so afraid. What made him change his mind and turn them down? No, never mind. It doesn't matter.''

Garret took a moment longer to enjoy her spontaneous burst of affectionate attention before grasping her shoulders and placing her at arm's length so he could continue. ''You haven't heard the rest.''

''You mean there's more?''

"He's selling half his interest in Big Salt to me."

Suddenly the smile on Laura's face felt terribly stiff. "Is that your idea of a joke?"

Garret felt his own pleasure evaporate. "I thought you'd be pleased. I think it's the perfect solution for all of us."

"But particularly for you?"

"Barnaby's in a financial bind, Laura. He's been doing his best to keep it from you and everyone else, but I went over some of his books this morning and the truth is if he doesn't do something soon, none of you will have a place to live."

"So, O'Keefe rides to the rescue."

"Damn it, Laura, you said yourself that this place is decaying. I can change that, but as it is it'll take me a good two years before I can get it operating in the black."

"I have every confidence in your abilities," she snapped back, reaching for her shirt. "The question is how? You see, I know how men like you operate, but I wonder if Barnaby does? You don't do anything strictly for charity, and you won't settle for simply building a flashy hotel, will you? You'll have to go the whole route—a casino, fancy restaurants. Don't forget the marina for those luxury yachts that are sure to come by."

"You're getting hysterical!"

"You bet I am!" She slid on her panties, almost tearing them in the process. "Do you see yourself as an *improvement*? These people deserve a chance to live better lives, but what are you going to offer them? Jobs as waitresses and waiters, maids and doormen. I can see lines forming already."

"It's a helluva lot more than they have right now."

"Things, Garret," she cried, whirling around in anger as he reached for his own clothes. "You can provide them with money to buy *things*. But who's going to build them the schools they need and the low-income housing? You don't make a profit on things like that so why should you care?''

"I care, Laura, but I'm not omnipotent. Grow up. Profit is what it's all about. My finance people already believe I've gone off the deep end. You know what I think this is really about?" he said, zipping up his shorts. "You're afraid that things will change all right—but for the better. You're afraid that these people might get to the point where they don't depend on the valiant, self-sacrificing Dr. Connell, and then this makeshift family you've created for yourself will be history."

"You bastard."

He finished slipping on his shirt, but left it unbuttoned, instead coming around the bed toward her. "Laura, don't. Don't let your own personal bitterness make you blind to the good side of practical business. I care for you. We could build something good here together."

She dropped back her head, laughing mirthlessly. "Of course. Why didn't I see it? You *do* have the whole thing figured out, don't you? All the way down to providing yourself with a cozy bed partner to while away those long empty evenings as you're building your new rich-man's playground."

Furious, Garret grabbed her by the shoulders. "That's not the way it is between us and you know it. We're two of a kind. We've been hurt and we're scarred, but when we're together none of that matters. We *belong* together, Laura." Crushing his mouth to hers he set out to prove it to her.

Gone was the kindness, the tenderness he'd shown her before. His mouth open, his fingers biting, he took her swiftly on a stomach-lurching ride to a place where storms were born and souls were lost. Fearless, determined, she closed her fingers around his shirt and dared him to show her more.

Reason left him, anger left him, and suddenly there was only Laura, filling his universe, filling his heart. God, he couldn't lose her now. He wouldn't!

"Tell me," he ground out. "Try and tell me this isn't real."

She didn't attempt to open her eyes, knowing the room would spin crazily if she did. "If you're finished I'd like you to leave now," she whispered, her throat painfully dry. She swallowed to ease the feeling. "Unless, of course, the clinic is part of your fifty percent."

She drew blood with that one. She didn't see it, but she felt it in the way his hold on her tightened. The marks would remain for days. Then suddenly she was free. Surprised, she opened her eyes to see him stalk toward the door and yank it open.

"The clinic remains yours," he said, his voice deceptively soft. "But you belong to me."

Ten

Though the changing of the seasons normally had little impact on Big Salt, fall's arrival promised to be memorable. But only as Laura turned her calendar from September to October did she realize *how* memorable.

The good news was that O'Keefe was gone. It was only temporary, she'd been told, but at this point any relief was better than none. However, even in his absence, upheaval on Big Salt continued, for he'd called in Giles to see that his instructions were carried out.

No matter where she went the buzz of excitement, concern and anticipation surrounded her. Everyone wanted to know what was going on. What did it mean for them? Why couldn't Barnaby tell them something concrete instead of giving them those empty assurances that everyone would be taken care of and that their lives would indeed soon improve? Every day scouts went to the far side of the island to see what would come of all the heavy equipment and building material piling up on the beach. And every movement was reported to the rest of the islanders and analyzed.

Laura didn't blame them for their discontent and worry, but she did her best to avoid getting directly involved in any of their debates. She had her own problems to contend with and her own future to start worrying about.

A few weeks after O'Keefe left she discovered fate had decided not to be lenient. She was pregnant.

In the back of her mind she'd known it would come to this. That morning after Lizzy's visit—when the reminder of her own folly struck its blow—she'd felt something, some tiny, vague difference. She'd managed to push the thought away, but no more. And never again would she doubt any woman who came to her to announce what doctors could only prove with tests.

Neither would she ever doubt that bad luck could be passed down from generation to generation.

For days she functioned in a trance. At night she couldn't sleep. She got to the point where she wondered if she wasn't losing her mind. Her only consolation was that O'Keefe was away; she had little doubt he would have noticed the state she was in, and then how long would it be before he put two and two together?

It wasn't that she didn't want children, she mused, she'd always dreamed of having them. But when her engagement ended, she'd put those dreams away. Now, at thirty-five, she wasn't sure she was still capable of tackling the responsibility. Granted, she was healthy, and women everywhere were proving it wasn't only acceptable, but safe to wait until their thirties to start families. Still, she wasn't sure she was up to it. She worried that she'd lost her resiliency and that wonderful sense of immortality the young possessed. She was also just plain scared.

But she knew that as long as she was certain her pregnancy was proceeding normally, she had to keep her baby. There were no other options—not for her. *That* choice had nothing to do with being a doctor and everything to do with realizing what her mother had gone through for *her*. In her most desperate moments, that knowledge gave her strength. Her mother had survived single parenthood and, somehow, she would, too.

However, just as her mind came to terms with her new condition, her body decided to test her durability. She began to feel lethargic and listless. She made a discreet trip to a doctor friend on Abaco to be doubly sure of her diagnosis and they agreed that vitamins would soon have her feeling better.

But no sooner was *that* problem taken care of then morning sickness hit with a vengeance.

She was feeling particularly miserable the morning she arrived at Whitehall to check in on Barnaby, who'd told her the day before that he was running low on his pills. The last thing she needed was to have him greet her at the door smoking one of Giles's cigars.

"I thought you'd agreed to follow my orders," she said, feeling her stomach roll as she entered the foyer and stepped into the trail of smoke that followed him like an accusing finger.

"I am." He thrust out his chest and thumped it with his free hand. "I haven't touched a drop of liquor before dinner in two weeks. Ask Sarah."

"I will. But I was referring to that," she said, indicating the expensive cigar with a derisive glance. "It isn't going to help your blood pressure, either."

He gave her a wheedling smile. "One little smoke a day? Have a heart, Laura. You said yourself that I was looking better."

So she did. Laura didn't know if it was Caleb's accident or his partnership with O'Keefe that had motivated this effort to pull himself together, but she had to admit it was one of the few changes she approved of these days. Still, why did he have to choose *now* to smoke the nasty thing? she thought, swallowing uneasily.

"Oh, all right," she muttered. "But *only* one. Promise?"

He laid his hand against his heart. "You have my word."

Not wanting to get into a discussion of the questionable value of *that*, she gestured for him to lead on. She followed him to the study, but was brought up short when she saw the extra tables lining the far wall. They were all cluttered, piled elbow high with stacks of books, folders and blueprints. "He doesn't believe in wasting any time, does he?"

"Not once he makes up his mind about something." Barnaby waved his cigar at the mess. "Though there are some wonderful ideas in all that. Big Salt is going to be everything I'd dreamed it could be. Care to take a peek?"

"No." Hearing the sharpness in her voice, she added more kindly, "I promised to finish reading the children *Robinson Crusoe* today. They're waiting for me."

Barnaby watched her go to the couch across the room and sit down. "Laura...you know I'd never intentionally stick my nose where it wasn't wanted."

"You're a worse busybody than old George."

He cleared his throat. "Yes, well, it *is* my island."

"I'm glad you're still able to believe that."

The elderly man frowned and came to sit down beside her. "I thought things had changed between you and O'Keefe." When she gave him a narrow-eyed look, he shrugged. "Well, I was sober enough to know he didn't come back to the house that night."

"That's just wonderful. Could we get on with this examination so I can leave?" she asked, feeling her own blood pressure begin to climb.

"Whatever this spat the two of you have had is, it's affected you deeply. You know I don't mean to be uncomplimentary, but you don't look well." He stroked his chin thoughtfully. "But for that matter, neither did *he* when he left." He reached over and patted her hands as they gripped her medical bag. "Laura, I know we've had our differences, but you're the closest thing to family I have and I can plainly see that something's not right."

"Everything is fine—at least it would be if I didn't have to inhale *that*," she muttered, looking pointedly at the half-smoked cigar.

"Oh, all right." He mournfully crushed the thing out in the crystal ashtray on the coffee table, and as she opened her bag to get her stethoscope and blood-pressure gauge, he released two more buttons on his short-sleeved shirt. "And I suppose if I invited you to join Giles and me for dinner tonight, you'd decline?"

"Probably."

Barnaby grunted his displeasure. "You're beginning to look as skinny as a runway model."

"Flattery will get you nowhere," she murmured dryly. But she smiled as she placed the stethoscope against his heart. "Deep breath, please. Hold. Exhale."

"I thought you at least liked *him*?"

"Once more, a deep breath. I do. Exhale."

"So join us for dinner. We're getting tired of having no one else but each other to face over the table every night. And he *never* lets me win at checkers the way you do."

Right now the last thing Laura wanted to talk about was food. Just the thought made her stomach queasier, and as she put away her stethoscope, she took a few discreet, stabilizing breaths.

After taking his blood pressure and commending him for his continued improvement, she gave him another month's supply of pills and tucked the rest of her things into her bag. The idea of getting some fresh air was becoming more necessary than appealing with every passing moment.

"You haven't answered me," Barnaby said, as she began to rise. "Tell you what. Come to dinner and I'll ask Sarah to prepare that shellfish terrine recipe Giles gave her."

Ordinarily Laura would have been amused—not to mention fascinated—to learn that Giles had any interest in cooking. But just picturing the process necessary to create that loaflike entrée, she felt the room spin and the feeling of nausea rise. As quickly as she'd stood up, she sat back down, then bent her head to her knees.

"Good lord, Laura. What is it?"

"Nothing. Give me a minute."

"Don't give me 'nothing'. Hold on. I'll go get Sarah."

"No!" She grabbed his arm to keep him from getting up. Sarah. That's all she needed. Not much escaped her kind, but shrewd, eyes. "It'll pass in a minute. I just need to take one or two of these, that's all."

Barnaby watched her reopen her bag and take out a small cellophane-wrapped package. "Crackers?" He grimaced. "In my opinion they're only good for helping ingest cheap paté or overcoming morning sickness, and you're not—''

When Laura glanced up, it was to see him staring at her with his mouth hanging wide open. She forced down the cracker that was sticking to the roof of her mouth. "All right already. Stop staring at me that way. You look like a grouper.''

"Is it true?" he asked in a hushed voice.

Knowing there was no point in denying it, she sighed. "I'm afraid so.''

"Oh, my. Why this is marvelous...simply marvelous.''

Laura's answering smile was grim. "That's easy for you to say.''

He was quickly apologetic. "Poor dear. I don't know much about, er, these things; however, I can see that it's not easy on you. But imagine...a baby.'' His face crinkled into a foolish smile. "Who else knows?''

"Absolutely *no one*, and I want you to swear you'll keep it that way,'' she replied, rewrapping her crackers and putting them away. She leaned back on the couch and, closing her eyes, willed the sickly feeling to pass.

Barnaby drew his eyebrows together in a worried frown. "Laura, you *are* going to tell O'Keefe, aren't you?''

It was the one thing she hadn't let herself think about. What would his reaction be? She was fairly certain he wouldn't question that the child was his, but she also didn't doubt he would be furious. It had been painfully clear that the only kind of relationship he was interested in was a physical one.

"I don't know,'' she murmured at last.

"But he has a right to know.''

"Maybe.''

Barnaby's frown turned into a full-fledged scowl. "You say that now, but what about in a few months when things are more—visible?"

She sat up, pressing a hand to her stomach. "I've been thinking about leaving."

"Ach—no."

The misery on his face was no less than she felt each time she forced herself to think of the wisdom of that solution. "It might be for the best. You said yourself that things are changing here."

"Yes, but we'll be needing the clinic more than ever, and the people trust you, Laura. They love you."

"I care for them, too, but now I have someone else to worry about than simply myself. I need to focus on providing for my baby."

"But O'Keefe would—"

"I don't want his money!"

"There, there, now." Barnaby patted her hand to try to calm her. "I'm going to go ask Sarah for something cool for you to drink. You rest a moment, and I'll be right back."

Despite her protests, he left and she sat there feeling miserable and foolish. It was a fine turn of events when the patient had to care for the doctor, she scolded herself, and all because of the mention of O'Keefe. If that wasn't enough to convince her the man was poison to her, she didn't know what was.

Taking a deep breath, she felt this latest wave of queasiness pass and carefully got up to cross over to the windows. Opening one of the latches, she pushed the hinged window out and drew in the scent of hibiscus and roses lingering in the back garden. Her thoughts drifted back to only a few short weeks ago when she'd stood out there and resisted the temptation to steal a few hours of pleasure with O'Keefe. She wondered if the pretty garden would be among the things he would change on Big Salt.

With a shake of her head, she turned away and her gaze fell on the table to her right. Too curious to resist, she stepped over to it and took a closer look at the rough sketch of what she recognized as the east beach. But what she didn't understand was the number of small, bungalow-type cottages sketched in instead of the one large hotel she'd expected.

"I thought you weren't interested?"

The familiar but unexpected voice gave her a start, and Laura turned to see Giles in the doorway grinning at her. His newly acquired tan brought out his jade-green eyes, which were glittering with pleasure at catching her. His words allowed her to overcome her own embarrassment and reply in kind. "I thought you were on the east beach playing lord high supervisor?"

"Alas, I'm expecting a call. But I *did* tell the wretches to keep their backs to it. You don't think I normally dress like this, do you?" he added, holding out his arms in invitation for her closer inspection.

Aware he knew she recognized a man most comfortable in three-piece suits when she saw one, Laura allowed herself to smile as she took in the olive green T-shirt and army fatigue pants that lent an intriguing quality to his elegant leanness. "I don't know...I think your tailor might be on to something."

"It's the physique," he said, giving her a wink as he came fully into the room. "I can't help but look good in everything."

"Ah. I hadn't noticed."

"The lady tramples over my ego ne'er knowing the damage she does." As he reached her, he picked up her hand and gallantly brought it to his lips. "But I'll forgive you if you tell me where you've been keeping yourself lately. I've been looking for you among our visitors—you know the ones who've been peeking between the bramble bushes spying on our progress?"

"We don't have bramble bushes on Big Salt, and don't pick on the islanders for being curious about what's going on. What you're doing might be small potatoes to you, but it means everything to them."

Giles whistled softly. "You *are* in a mood, aren't you?" He slipped his arm around her shoulder and studied her with more concern. "You're pale, as well. Are you feeling ill?"

"Don't you start, too. Barnaby's already trying to mother me. It's nothing but fatigue—and I'm sorry if I sounded curt. I know none of this is your fault," she said, sweeping her hand toward the tables.

"Ah-ha. Now I follow. You're still intent on burning O'Keefe in effigy." Giles went over to the nearest table and tossed down the blueprint he'd been carrying, before turning to give her a rueful smile. "Laura, love, I thought you were more fair than that. Here you are judging the man, and you don't even know what his plans are."

"No one knows his plans except you and maybe Barnaby. *That's* the problem. When he stands before the whole population and explains himself, then maybe I'll feel less antagonistic toward him."

"He will. But not until he's about to do something that he feels will affect them. At this point, nothing we're doing does."

"*He feels?* You're going to be bringing hundreds of tourists to the island and you don't think that will affect them?"

"Hundreds?" This time it was Giles's turn to look confused. "Only a few dozen at a time, I assure you. He knows the island's too small to cope with the larger venture those other investors wanted." Giles followed her gaze as it dropped down to the blueprints she'd been looking at when he entered. "Come see for yourself. These are small bungalows. We'll be catering to the discriminating vacationer who's as eager to maintain his privacy as the islanders are to keep theirs."

Laura inched closer to take a better look. The drawings began to make more sense now and she could follow the artist's concept, saw that the thatch-roofed buildings would stand on stilts—protected against high water and unwelcome visits of Butch's "crawlies"—and blend in attractively with the palm trees and surrounding vegetation. "They look like something from a Tarzan movie."

"I was thinking more in the line of 'unpretentious but serene' for our ads. You'd be surprised how many chief-executive types jump at the chance to simply disappear for a few days of complete relaxation." Giles gave her a sidelong look. "Is this more acceptable to you?"

"You know it is." The look she shot back at him was reproachful, even as it was apologetic. "But this reestablishes what I said before. If the islanders knew about this, they'd be less inclined to feel they need to keep an eye on you."

"I see what you mean. But look at it from our point of view. If I showed them this, they'd ask what comes next, and we're not at the point where we've decided that in our own minds."

"I think this has more to do with O'Keefe's preferring to operate the way most bureaucracies do—everything is on a 'need to know' basis, and the peons don't need to know."

Giles grinned, unabashed. "I didn't say O'Keefe wanted to turn this into a complete democracy." Just as quickly, he grew serious. "But he's a fair man, Laura. He wants Barnaby and everyone to be able to live with these plans. *You* most of all."

"He's certainly going about it strangely," she replied, though she told herself she was referring to the former part of that remark. However, Giles read her better than she wanted to admit.

"Yes, well, as I've more or less told you before, until you came along, he's never had to try to impress a woman."

"I don't want to be impressed. I want to be left alone."

"Do you?" Giles gave her a crooked smile, though she was busily inspecting her cuticles. "Strange, *he* said much the same thing the day he left—right after I caught him watching you from his bedroom window. I wonder how long it's going to take before the two of you figure out what it is you really want?"

Her head snapped up. "What are you talking about?"

"You're in love with him."

"Are you—"

Before Laura could finish the phone rang. As she spun around, she nearly knocked an antique sextant off the edge of Barnaby's desk. A combination cellular and microwave phone system was the first thing O'Keefe had insisted they install, and this was the first time Laura had heard it work. That was the only reason she'd overreacted—or so she told herself. When Giles picked up the receiver and her suspicions of who was on the other end of the line were confirmed, she knew the real reason.

Her heart began to pound. Her palms were instantly wet. She stood very still, hoping by some stroke of luck Giles would forget she was there. After their initial greeting, they'd immediately began talking business and she thought her wish would be realized—Giles told Garret he was going to put him on the intercom and look up something for him. She eased around to the front of the desk to get further out of the way.

"I thought you'd be on your way back by now," Giles called over his shoulder, as he dug into a stack of papers on one of the tables.

"So did I," Garret replied, his deep, rich voice vibrating through the room. "But as usual there's a snag or two. How're things going over there?"

"Well, this isn't Club Med, but it has its charms."

Laura heard O'Keefe's sharp intake of breath.

"English, I'm tired, I'm ticked off, and I've got two more hellish meetings to get through before I can hop a plane out of here. This is no time to get my juices stirred any more than they already are. Now we had an agreement. You'd keep your aristocratic tail away from her, you—"

"Calm down, old man. You know what your problem is? You have a one-track mind these days."

"Tell me something I don't know."

"What I'm trying to say is that if your language gets any more colorful, you're going to embarrass the lovely lady standing here."

Laura waved her hands and shook her head, but it was already too late. She knew it by the silence that began to throb in the room, or was that her heartbeat echoing in her ears?

"Laura."

She'd heard him say her name before in anger and laughter, and more than once in passion. But never with the wistfulness of someone who felt abysmally alone and yearned for that loneliness to be over. It wrenched at her heart and threatened to turn her limbs to jelly. To keep from giving herself away, she raised her clasped hands and pressed them to her lips.

Garret exhaled, the sound weary. "Laura, please say something."

She wanted to. Her heart cried yes, but her mind held her back. Whatever that wild, wonderful thing was that had been between them, it was over. It had to be. The baby came first now.

She backed over to the coffee table and picked up her bag. Garret must have heard her footsteps because his agitation was quick and sharp.

"Damn it. Don't walk out on me. Laura! Channing!" Static obliterated the expletive that followed. "*Do* something."

Laura didn't hang around to see if Giles would follow his boss's orders, and nearly knocked Barnaby down as she ran into the foyer. The last thing she heard as she reached for the door was Giles telling Garret he believed they'd both done enough for one day.

Laura wasn't sure how she made it back to the clinic without breaking her neck. The tears that began spilling from her eyes all but blinded her. She was only grateful that she didn't meet anyone along the way.

If she'd had any doubts about the wisdom of going, they were gone. She had to leave the island. She had a little money saved; she would go back to the States, head west, maybe start fresh. The one thing she wouldn't do, she vowed, was denigrate her child by continuing her affair with O'Keefe—and if she stayed, she knew that's what would happen. The sheer force of the intense sexuality between them assured it. Yet that wasn't the only reason; she was beginning to understand that, too.

Dear God, she thought, when had she fallen in love with him?

Eleven

Garret sat at the makeshift table under the open-walled tent and glared holes into the back of the man walking away. That took care of that, he told himself with grim pleasure. If he wanted all the bungalows to have sky-lights over the beds in the master bedrooms, then they would have them. He didn't care if it *did* mean losing a week's worth of work and more money.

"Fool," he muttered, as the man disappeared around a small mountain of lumber. Garret reached for the bottle of whiskey beside him and refilled his empty glass, his mood turning more morose. It seemed it was his lot to be surrounded by fools these days, and why not when he was feeling like the king of them all?

Four days...four days he'd been back on Big Salt and she still wouldn't speak to him. He'd tried everything short of groveling, but, no, the good doctor would have none of it or him. She'd even taken to locking her doors to keep him away!

Women. Whatever had made him think he *wanted* to try to understand them? He was beginning to wonder if his father had been right when he'd advocated enjoying them, but never making the mistake of losing your head over one. Only it was too late for him, and he didn't know what to do about it. Almost. With his next sip of whiskey, he thought about his latest retaliation and took solace in it.

She was applying for a job back in the States. Running away from him, is how he saw it. He'd discovered the news when he found her mail in the box in Barnaby's foyer, the one the supply boat picked up and carried to Abaco twice a week. Without an ounce of conscience, he'd opened one of the letters, calling his action justified when he'd realized the letter was a job résumé. It also didn't sit well with him that he'd learned more about her from those few sheets of paper than he had in the two months he'd known her. As a result he tore up the entire batch, then soothed his temper and despair by imagining her reaction when her efforts yielded no responses. Why, he rationalized, should he be the only one going out of his mind?

He was still brooding about that when Giles and Barnaby came over. They eyed the dent in the bottle before exchanging speaking glances.

"Can anyone join this wake or is it by invitation only?" Giles asked, gesturing to Barnaby to take the steel folding chair while he pulled over an empty wooden crate for himself.

Garret leaned back and clasped his hands over his taut stomach. "Let me guess—Walker has been crying on your shoulders, and you want to plead his case against the skylights for him?''

"It's not that you don't have the right to change your mind," Giles replied, ignoring his sarcasm. "But it gets a bit wearing on the nerves when it becomes an hourly routine."

"You're breaking my heart." Garret shoved the bottle toward him. "Forget Walker and have a drink."

With a philosophical shrug, Giles hunted down two coffee mugs and poured himself and Barnaby a drink. Barnaby—reluctant but conscientious—poured half of his back into Giles's cup and diluted the rest with ice water from a cooler.

"Waste of good whiskey," Garret grumbled.

"But not worth inviting one of Laura's lectures."

"If you don't mind, under my roof—" he glanced up as a gust of wind pulled at the canvas "—such as it is, the good doctor is a forbidden subject."

"You mean all deals are off?" Giles said, already rising from his chair.

"Put it down, English. I didn't say anything of the kind." Garret took another drink. "I've lost a skirmish or two, not the war."

"That's a unique way of putting it," Giles replied, his tone mocking. "Are we talking about a hostile takeover or winning the eternal affections of a woman?"

"Let's put it this way: losing in anything doesn't interest me."

"That's the attitude," Barnaby said, lifting his glass in salute. "Don't give up, O'Keefe. I have confidence you'll win her yet."

"Not the way *he's* going about it," Giles drawled. At Garret's dark scowl, he smiled innocently and took a long sip of his own drink.

"Let's just change the subject," Garret said. But after a few more moments of silence asked, "What's wrong with the way I'm going about it?"

"Well, for one thing—to borrow from a very old guidebook, 'love is kind....'"

"It's *bloody* hard to be kind when she's turning my life inside out."

Giles turned to Barnaby. "Amazing, isn't it? Have you ever met two people who were better matched, but less communicative?" He turned back to Garret. "Why the devil don't you simply go to her and tell her you're in love with her? She's a lovely, reasonable woman."

"Because lovely, reasonable Laura would as soon cut off my nose with one of her scalpels as look at me."

"It makes one wonder. Whatever did you do?"

"Nothing," Garret growled. Then he grimaced. "What was wrong with telling her I wanted to take care of her, buy her a few luxuries?"

Giles drew his finger down the side of his nose. "Ah, yes. What independent woman could resist the offer to be treated like a bedouin chieftain's houri?"

"That's *not* the way I meant it."

"But undoubtedly *that's* the way she took it. Wouldn't a proposal have been far more indicative of your—er, affections?"

"I thought we were working up to it."

"I suppose you *can* reach Hawaii by way of the North Pole."

"Go to hell."

"What you need is leverage," Barnaby mused, stroking his chin. "Say...if she was pregnant. You want an heir, don't you, O'Keefe?"

He wanted Laura more. Garret shook his head, the liquor he'd consumed slowing his mental processes. "You forget who Laura is—if anyone would be determined to raise a child alone, it's her. Besides, how am I supposed to attain point B if I can't reach point A?''

Barnaby dismissed that with a wave of his hand. ''Women love romance. They dream of a hero to carry them off and tell them how things are going to be.''

Giles choked on his drink. ''Now hold on a moment—''

''Wait!'' Garret shot up out of his chair, almost knocking his own drink over. ''I think he might be on to something!''

Giles gave him an incredulous look. ''Just remember, there's only one doctor on this island, and if she's wanted for attempted murder, you won't want to be on her operating table.''

''What do I have to lose?''

Giles rolled his eyes before dropping his head in his hand. As Garret set off for the small pickup truck they'd had shipped to the island, Giles heard Barnaby chuckle. ''Do you know what you've done?''

''Of course. I've told the truth without breaking a confidence.''

''Care to interpret that?''

''You'll see, old chap, you'll see.... If he doesn't drive that thing into a ditch first.''

Laura led the children in another chorus of ''Row Row Row Your Boat'' while burping Lizzy's baby. Instead of glancing at her watch, she noted the sun's position and mentally gauged that it was about time for everyone to make their way home for dinner.

Across from her, she saw Caleb sitting under Uncle George's favorite shade tree with George and a few of the other elders. Speculating, she mused. She imagined there hadn't been so much to talk about since the arrival of the first Tremaines.

She was glad when she saw Caleb burst into laughter. At first she'd worried about his psychological recovery—he was such a proud man—but he was going to be all right, especially since the hospital on Abaco had informed her that they had a sponsor to help get him an artificial limb and therapy to learn to use it.

The baby wriggled restlessly, and Laura kissed the coal-black fuzz on top of her head before turning her so she could see the children singing. "Okay," she said, when the song became impossibly muddled. "That's enough. It's time to call it a day."

"We wanna play ring de rosie," one child called, and others agreed with a loud cheer.

"'Ring Around the Rosie,'" Laura said, patiently correcting her. "All right, but you have to play alone, because I'm holding the baby."

As the children jumped up and began linking hands, Laura's attention was caught by two boys running toward them in the distance. It was Shrimp and Angel. The younger boy went straight to his father while Angel came to her.

"Doc, you gotta come quick. Deys taking down the cane shed."

"Who?"

"Two men. Say dey got orders from Mr. O'Keefe."

Laura compressed her lips into a grim line. "Is that so? Well, we'll see about that."

She took the baby in to Lizzy, quickly explaining why she had to leave. When she came back outside, Caleb and several others stood with the boys, ready to accompany her.

"Doc, how can dis be?" Caleb asked her.

"I don't know, but we're going to find out."

They hurried along the dirt road, between tall rows of cane that had yet to be harvested. When they rounded the bend and saw the shed, there were already a number of people grouped there shouting protests and questions. Laura and her companions eased their way to the center of the group where two men stood looking as if they wished they could be anywhere but there. When they saw her, their expression indicated they clearly thought she was there to support them.

"Dr. Connell, can you explain to these people that we're just here to do our job?"

"And what exactly is that, Mr.—Banks, isn't it?" she said, struggling to remember, since she'd only seen the man once before at Barnaby's.

"Yes, ma'am. We've been told to come over here and take a look at this place to decide what equipment we'll need to take it down."

"Why take it down?"

"I don't know, ma'am, er, Doctor. I just know O'Keefe said it's got to come down."

"But that's insane. These people need to work in here. There's machinery.... How are they supposed to process the cane? No, don't tell me," she said, as the man opened his mouth to speak. "You don't know. You just have your orders."

"I'm sorry."

"No, *I'm* sorry, Mr. Banks, because I'm going to have to ask you to leave. No one is going to tear down anything until O'Keefe himself gives these people a good reason why."

The man ran a hand over his hair and looked at her compassionately. "Doctor, I don't know if you want to do that. Last I heard he wasn't in a pretty mood."

"Neither am I."

She walked alone and fast. With every step her temper heated until it was as sizzling as the sun penetrating through her shirt. A lizard dashed between her feet, but she never saw it; her gaze was centered on Whitehall, and her thoughts on the man who had pushed too far this time.

The absence of vehicles out front only intensified her mood, but she didn't care if he was on the other side of the island. They were going to have this out once and for all.

Just as she was about to take the cutoff that circled the mansion and led to the east beach, she saw O'Keefe's new truck coming around from the opposite side of the house. But the better news was that O'Keefe was driving. Though not well, she thought with a sniff as she watched the white truck overshoot the turn and make a wide loop across the front lawn.

He parked, got out, and headed straight toward her, his head slightly lowered. She felt a tingling sensation rush through her and quickly assured herself that it was nothing more than adrenaline. She wouldn't let his majestic good looks get to her, or the determined glint she saw in his own eyes.

"I want to talk to you," she began, when they were still yards apart. "I want to know why—" As he swooped her up and tossed her over his right shoulder, her world was turned upside down and she shrieked in surprise. *"Garret!"*

"Nice of you to remember my name," he replied, doing an about-face and heading for the stairs.

Laura's cry of indignation was cut off when her insides protested violently at this sudden assault, and she had to gulp several times to keep down her meager lunch. "Are you mad? Put me down."

"Not on your life."

"It'll be *your* life, if you don't put me down this instant."

Instead he climbed the stairs and carried her into the house. Blood was rushing into her head and with every step he took, she felt dizzier. She tried to raise herself by bracing her hands on his back, but he turned to shut the front door behind himself and she lost her balance.

"O'Keefe, you—" Unable to think of a suitable insult, she beat her clenched fists against his back, but she might as well have been beating on a teak statue. His muscular back absorbed the blows, and he only laughed.

"Don't hurt yourself, sweetheart."

Hearing the slight slur of his words, her rage intensified. "You're drunk!"

"Not quite."

"You are so, and if you think I'm going to have anything to do with you when you're in this condition, you're sorely mistaken. Oh, God! Not the stairs! Where are you taking me? You'll kill us both."

As Garret started up the wide staircase, Sarah came rushing into the foyer to see what all the commotion was about. When she saw them, she came to an abrupt halt and stared openmouthed. Garret gave her a friendly grin.

"Afternoon, Sarah. Hold dinner for a few hours, would you?"

"Sarah!" Laura brushed her braid out of her face so she could see her. "Sarah—oh, thank goodness—go get help. Hurry!"

"Step foot out of this house," Garret warned, "and you're fired."

"*You* can't fire her," Laura snapped.

"I just gave her a raise. If I can do the one, I don't see why I can't do the other."

He carried her down the hallway to his bedroom, but when he tried to take her inside, he discovered she'd grabbed hold of the doorjamb and refused to let go. Muttering something she couldn't quite make out, he shifted his hold to force her to relax her grip.

"I don't want to hurt you."

"I'm not going in there."

"It's the only way." The words were growled as he broke her hold and pulled her inside. The sound of the slamming of the door echoed in the otherwise silent house.

A moment later, Laura found herself on her feet and pressed against the door by Garret's strong body. There was no mistaking his intentions and she pushed frantically against his chest while turning her head to avoid his kisses.

"Not again. No more," she cried.

"You don't mean that. You were coming to the house to look for me."

"To *talk*."

"I'm tired of talking. Things always get turned around when we talk." He traced the delicate outer shell of her ear with his tongue before nipping at her lobe. "Laura, I miss you. I need you."

She closed her eyes against the sexy persuasion of his voice. "I won't let you do this to me. I only came to talk to you about the cane shed. Stop that!" She slapped at his hands as he brushed her collar aside to place a love bite at the base of her neck. "Why are you pulling it down?"

"Because I like the way you taste there."

"I *meant* the shed. Garret, please. You need some coffee, and I need to sit down." Whenever she tried to focus on anything, the room began to spin and that awful nausea returned. She couldn't bear the thought of becoming ill in front of him, and resisted the most frustrating urge to start crying, the same way she fought back the pleasure that surged to the surface whenever, wherever he touched her. She told herself it was only due to the changes in her body; but crazy hormones or not, she wasn't going to cry over him again. Only when she felt him fumbling with her belt and the clasp of her pants did she stop caring about embarrassing herself in front of him.

"What are you doing?" she gasped, trying to twist away.

"Making you pregnant." But her zipper had become stuck and he scowled down at it as if it had done it intentionally.

"You big jerk, *I am pregnant!*"

He thought the announcement, shrieked in his ear, was enough of a big blow to bowl him over. When she followed it with a hammering punch to his chest, she gave him another. Doubled over and gasping for breath, because she'd zeroed in near one of his still sensitive ribs, he watched her clutch her own stomach before racing past him. If he'd had any doubts about what she'd said, they were soon dispelled when he heard her in the bathroom.

Stupefied, he went in after her and poured himself a glass of water and then another and another. Never in the history of fermented grain products had sobriety come more quickly.

"Give me that," Laura muttered, joining him at the sink and taking the glass from him. "I need it more than you do."

She looked feverish, glassy eyed, and thoroughly miserable. Garret wanted to take her in his arms and rock her until all the hurt went away; instead, he wet the fresh washcloth lying on the counter and began to bathe her face with it. At first she resisted, but he was persistent.

"Hush. I only want to help you."

"If you meant that, you'd get out of my life and leave me in peace."

He braced himself against the pain that inevitably produced and rinsed out the washcloth. "You're carrying my child."

"*My* child."

"Ours, then."

It sounded so... permanent that she had to turn her head away to hide the yearning in her eyes. "Could I have a minute alone?"

"Of course."

He stepped out, closing the door behind him, and began pacing—as much to work off more of the alcohol in his system as to kill time. *A baby.* The thought ran over and over again in his head. He was going to be a father. He felt a giddy sense of joy, a quiet sense of awe, and then a feeling he would have preferred never experiencing again—despair.

When the door to the bathroom opened a few minutes later, he was standing squarely before it like a sentry. "When were you going to tell me?"

"I wasn't."

His chest rose and fell on a deep breath. It hurt; even though he expected the answer, it hurt. He wanted to ask why, but the question was locked in his throat.

She saw it and struggled against doubt and hope. "I thought you would think it was my fault."

Ahh. A flicker of confidence rekindled in him. This he could understand. This he could deal with, overcome. He took a step closer. "I was there. Remember?"

"It was a passionate moment. We weren't thinking."

"On the contrary I knew very well who I was stepping into that shower with." He took another step closer. "The question is, why did you let me?"

She moistened her dry lips. "That's not fair and you know it."

"All right. The second time then? And the third? And the time after that scene on the beach?"

"Since when have you ever taken 'no' for an answer?"

"*Always*...until I met a woman who made me feel things I'd never felt before, want things I didn't know existed, dream of things I thought out of reach." He tried to soothe her with the gentle rumble of his voice and when he was near enough, he reached out and stroked his fingers down the length of her arm.

Laura stepped back, but found herself against the bathroom door. In defense she lifted her chin. "You don't have to try to seduce me again. I admit I was wrong. I won't deny you your visitation rights."

"Damn the visitation rights!" he growled, grasping her arms and nearly lifting her off her feet. "Do you love me or don't you?"

"Garret—you're hurting me."

As quickly as his temper flared, it deflated and, uttering a soft oath, he swept her into his arms and carried her over to the bed. He laid her down and stretched out beside her. "I'm sorry," he whispered, brushing tender kisses over her cheek, her forehead. "I'm so sorry. I seem destined to always make the wrong moves with you, but don't you understand, Laura? It's because you're who you are that I don't know how to go about things. I've never been in love before. I'm clumsy. I feel like a boy with his first crush." He kissed her again, but on the lips.

Laura felt her response, despite her good intentions, then turned her head away. "Oh, Garret, it's no good. We don't communicate except in bed. You're so used to getting anything you want. You don't negotiate—you reach out and snatch."

"So teach me."

"We haven't got that much time."

Humor lit his eyes. "Wanna bet?"

As he kissed her again, this time more insistently, Laura felt her resolve weakening. Dear God, she adored him. How could she think life would be anything more than existing without him? Yes, he was arrogant and, yes, he was overwhelming, but he possessed her heart. What could she do?

"Tell me again," she whispered, sliding her hands up his chest and linking them around his neck.

"Let me show you. Let me spend the rest of my life showing you."

They came together for a kiss that was tender even in its urgency. With their fingertips, they traced each other's faces, gentling the flash of need the deep kiss inspired. *Slowly,* they entreated by touch, *we have the rest of our lives*.

She was so soft, he reveled in rediscovery, exploring her, drawing her wild-honey taste deep within himself. Between kisses, he whispered to her, telling of nights of torment when he'd been alone, and the memories of loving her had come back to haunt him. "I want to see you," he whispered, reaching for her buttons.

They undressed each other, smiling, caressing, pressing together to relish the simple joy of touching. Her loss of weight brought him anguish. Her swelling breasts enchanted him. But when he pressed his lips to her stomach, it was *her* eyes that filled with tears.

"How do you feel?" he wondered aloud.

Blinking furiously, she smiled. "Very sexy."

He eased up to cover her with his body and slowly began to claim a place for himself within her, watching what it did to her in the dilation of her eyes. He exhaled shakily and buried his face against her neck. "Don't let me wake up and discover this is a dream. Oh, God, Laura, love me. Just love me."

Feeling her own ecstasy shimmering through her, she drew him closer and answered the throbbing thrust of his body with her own. *Always,* her heart promised. *Always.*

Long afterward, they were still touching, caressing each other, and they knew it wouldn't be long before things intensified again. But as Garret enjoyed this newfound contentment, he was also aware that though Laura was with him in love, she still had doubts about their future. Raising himself on his elbow, he started what was fast becoming a favorite pastime; he began to unbraid her hair.

"Do you want to finish chewing me out now?"

"Oh, Garret—see what you do to me?" She closed her eyes in mortification. "It's a wonder there isn't a lynch mob out front."

"Why? Because I wanted to take down that cane shed?" he asked, trying to recall what the fuss was all about. "Sweetheart, it's archaic, dangerous, and it has to come down if I'm to put in the small cannery. They'll have their precious cane press, but I guarantee you it'll be one that's safer to be around."

She focused only on what he'd first said. "A cannery? You're going to put in a *cannery*?"

"Among other things. I'll show you." Rolling off the bed, he went into the bathroom and came right back out, dragging on a white terry cloth robe. Seeing she was still lying there staring at him, he grinned and, wrapping her in the bedspread, swept her into his arms.

"What are you doing now? Garret, you can't—"

But he could and did. He carried her downstairs and into the study to the cluttered tables, where he set her on her feet and proceeded to show her his plans.

"This is the cannery here, nothing too overwhelming—just enough to meet the needs of the island's produce production. Over here are the hydroponic gardens."

"Hydro—what?"

"Drip irrigation that has a number of nutrients added to the water. It drips into each plant pot. I've seen it work on other islands with incredible success. The Tremaines were right in naming this place the way they did, but I doubt they realize *how* right. We have some of the best water around coming out of our springs. It's about time we use it."

"What's this down here by the bungalows?"

"A combination marina, restaurant, and souvenir stand." He gave her a sheepish grin. "I thought we'd promote a few cottage industries."

She pointed to the small building on the other side of the clinic. "And this?"

"That's the new school," Garret said quietly. "It was supposed to be a surprise."

Laura pretended to study the drawings with more interest, while fighting her latest impulse to start crying. Pregnancy, she decided, was certainly hard on the tear ducts. She cleared her throat. "It looks like you have everything figured out."

Garret reached out to stroke her hair. "I know what you're thinking. I should have told you sooner, explained to the others what I was up to. But understand this. When I decided to make a counteroffer to the one that group made Barnaby, I knew only two things: one was that he was near bankruptcy and if he lost Big Salt, you and everyone you cared for lost, too; and the other thing was that I'd just shared the most incredible night of my life with a woman who took my breath away." He shrugged and tried to cover his tension by smiling. "I was trying to be noble and romantic. In both cases I was groping in the dark and I guess I blew it."

Laura bit her lip in dismay. "I thought it was all an ego trip for you, that you only wanted me as your mistress."

"You're my *life*," Garret said, his voice certain and strong as he tossed the drawings back on the table and drew her into his arms. "When are you going to believe that?"

"Right after you take me upstairs and prove it," she whispered against his lips.

Epilogue

I haven't given birth to a son. I've borne a grizzly cub," Laura murmured dryly as she held her newborn in her arms for the first time.

"Nine pounds. Now there's a healthy lad," Barnaby said, puffed up like a proud rooster.

Laura smiled down at the golden blond fuzz covering the well-formed head. "He looks just like his father."

"No beard yet," Garret teased, reaching over to stroke the little one's chubby cheek. He wasn't surprised to see that his hand wasn't quite steady. It had been a miraculous evening and he still couldn't quite believe that they were now a family of three. Four, considering that Barnaby had insisted they move into the mansion and was already claiming kinship to the child to anyone who would listen. As he lifted his gaze, he met Laura's serene eyes and knew she was thinking much the same thing.

They had a great deal to be thankful for. Over the past several months they'd accomplished many of their goals. Some new ones were on the drawing board, and if some of the islanders still seemed a bit cautious around Garret, they were more than willing to defer to Laura's judgment and give him the benefit of the doubt. At least *he* was beginning to understand her deep affection for them.

"Yes, indeed," Barnaby continued. "A few more like him and you'll have the beginnings of a dynasty."

"Mr. Tremaine!" Mrs. Shaughnessy, the matronly nurse Garret had flown in on Giles's recommendation, swept into the room. She gave him her most imperious look, and though they were of equal height and similar portly proportions, he cringed noticeably. "Mrs. O'Keefe is barely through with birthing the wee babe and already you're wishing her with child again? Take a look, Mr. Tremaine. That's a woman you have there, not prize breeding stock. It's clear you've been away from genteel folk far too long."

Barnaby rolled his eyes at Garret. "I've no doubt you'll do your best to correct the situation, you old crone."

"What's that?"

"I said, I meant it with the utmost respect, ma'am," he quickly replied, turning to give her a formal bow.

But Mrs. Shaughnessy was not quite the deaf dimwit he'd hoped. "Pagan," she spat, giving him a push toward the door. "Now get on with you, so the lady can get some rest." Clucking in dismay, she turned to Laura. "It's time you get some sleep, child. It won't be long before that one awakes squalling for his first meal."

Laura smiled at the endearment, then looked wistfully down at her son. "Oh, Martha. Just a few minutes more? I'm really not that tired and—he's so *new*."

The cherub-faced woman melted like the wax on a Christmas candle. "Tsk . . . fifteen minutes then." She turned away to dab at her eyes and saw Barnaby still watching from the threshold. "And what do you think you're doing loitering about?" The rest of her tirade was muffled by the door as she closed it behind her.

Laura chuckled softly. "I don't think Barnaby is ever going to forgive Giles for recommending her. Do you really think she was the nanny to the earl's children?"

Garret lifted an eyebrow in mock arrogance. "Would I hire anyone but the best to look after you and my son?"

Smiling, Laura bent to brush her lips across her child's forehead for the dozenth time. "Hello, Garret Edmund O'Keefe II. Welcome to our life. Oh, Garret, look. He's smiling."

Garret shifted so he could hold her and the baby in his arms and kissed her own sweat-damp hair. "Sweetheart, I never thought I'd hear a *doctor* say anything quite as adorable. Are you sure you're feeling all right?"

He still couldn't believe that the child in their arms had emerged from her womb. He'd stayed with her throughout her labor and there were times when he'd been ready to panic.

"I'm fine." She laid her head against his shoulder. "Which reminds me, don't you think it's about time you sent that emergency helicopter back, before the storm hits?"

On cue, a rumble of thunder echoed in the distance. It reminded Garret of another storm a year earlier that had brought him to this place and this love. "In a minute I'll go tell him to shut down and take one of the guest rooms." He laid his cheek against Laura's hair. "Happy?"

"Incredibly. I love you."

Garret lifted her chin so he could look into her eyes. "And I love you."

"Wait until Giles hears."

"Serves him right for thinking he could fly to New York and deliver that contract before the baby came."

"We need to wire Mo."

"I already made the call."

Laura stretched to kiss his cheek. "Thank you for agreeing to put him through school. He's going to be a wonderful doctor." Another stronger rumble of thunder sounded. "It's going to be a big storm," she murmured.

"Let it come. Twice now you've proven to me that good things can come from them, Doc...Mrs. O'Keefe."

"The pirate's lady," she mused. "We did well today, didn't we? Maybe our son will grow up to be a celebrated surgeon."

"Are you kidding? Look at those paws. He's going to be all thumbs...but smart. See his eyes? He'll be an attorney or a judge."

"In any event, he'll be gorgeous. Poor darling. Women will throw themselves at him."

"His father will teach him to wait for the right one."

"Good thing, too," Laura said, laughing and reaching up to touch her husband's cheek. "It might be the only way I get another doctor in the family."

When Martha Shaughnessy reentered the room a half hour later, it was to find the three of them asleep. She carefully lifted the baby out of Laura's arms, but as she reached to turn out the light on the nightstand she found herself looking straight into Garret's pale blue eyes.

"Take care of him, Martha."

"And you your lady, sir."
"It's a deal. Good night, Martha. God bless."
"He already has, sir."

* * * * *